QUERP: BESTIARY

CREDITS

QUERP created by Shane Garvey

Author:
Shane Garvey and Jamie Wallis

layout & Graphic Design & Final Illustrations:
Jamie Wallis

Illustrations:
Martin Mckenna; Cindi L; Andreas Meyer;
Jeffrey Collingwood; Johannes Wiebel; Mark William Penny;
pzAxe; Ralf Juergen Kraft; Jamie Wallis; Sinisa Botas; Algol;
Drazen Vukelic & Linda Bucklin.

All character names and place names in this book are fictional. Any resemblance to actual persons or places is purely coincidental.

www.greywoodpublishing.com

QUERP: BESTIARY

Published by Greywood Publishing
www.greywoodpublishing.com

First Edition Print: July 2008
Second Edition Print: Dec 2010

ISBN: 9780955985508

QUERP: Quick Easy Role Playing
is © copyright 2010 Greywood Publishing

Text is © copyright 2010 Shane Garvey & Jamie Wallis

Trade dress, QUERP Logo, Greywood Publishing Logo
& cover design are © copyright 2010
Greywood Publishing

Images are © copyright their respective owners.

No part of this book may copied or reproduced with
prior written permission of the the copyright holders

Table of Contents

Introduction	4	Giant	41	Ogre	73
		Giant Bat	42	Orc	74
Angel	6	Giant Centipede	43	Panther	75
Assassin	7	Giant Eagle	44	Pegasus	76
Bandit	8	Giant Rat	45	Phoenix	77
Banshee	9	Giant Scorpion	46	Pixie	78
Basilisk	10	Giant Snake	47	Rakshasa	79
Bear	11	Giant Spider	48	Satyr	80
Beastman	12	Giant Wolf	49	Sea Serpent	81
Black Knight	13	Gnome	50	Skeleton	82
Boar	14	Goblin	51	Slaver	83
Brownie	15	Golem	52	Soldier	84
Carnivorous Plant	16	Gorgon	53	Sphinx	85
Caveman	17	Gorilla	54	Tiger	86
Catoblepas	18	Griffon	55	Titan	87
Centaur	19	Harpy	56	Treeman	88
Chimera	20	Hell Hound	57	Troll	89
Cockatrice	21	Hippogriff	58	Unicorn	90
Crocodile	22	Hobgoblin	59	Vampire	91
Cyclops	23	Horse	60	Warhound	92
Demon	24	Hydra	61	Werewolf	93
Doppelganger	25	Kobold	62	Will-o'-the-Wisp	94
Dragon	26	Kraken	63	Wolf	95
Dragonman	30	Leprechaun	64	Wraith	96
Dryad	31	Leviathan	65	Wyvern	97
Dwarf	32	Lich	66	Yeti	98
Eagle	33	Lion	67	Zombie	99
Elemental	34	Mammoth	68		
Elf	36	Manticore	69	Appendix I	100
Gargoyle	37	Merman	70	Appendix II	106
Genie	38	Minotaur	71		
Ghoul	40	Nymph	72		

Introduction

Welcome to the first QUERP supplement – The QUERP BESTIARY.

Within this tome you will find every creature that you will need to stock out your dungeon and wilderness QUERP adventures. If it crawls, bites, spits, flies, breathes fire, fights dirty or can turn you to stone... you will find it in here.

Quite simply, this book expands upon and revises the Fantasy Monsters chapter of the QUERP Rulebook. The monsters found within that book are also listed here, though they have been updated and expanded to follow the new monster conventions used for the Bestiary. In these cases, you should use the monsters as presented here rather than in the rulebook.

Disclaimer

This is not a standalone book. This book requires the QUERP, Quick Easy Role Play, Rulebook as published by Greywood Publishing (ISBN: 978-0-9559855-0-8).

How to Use This Book

As the cover title suggests, this book is crammed to the hilt with monsters and enemies. The monsters have been alphabetically categorised to help you choose the right monster for your adventure. In addition, at the back of the book you will find them listed by Native Terrain, Creature Type and Threat Level.

The Monster Description

Below is a breakdown of the monster (we use the term monster as a general description for everything that isn't human... and some things that are!) statistic descriptions.

Creature Description

Here you will find a detailed description of what the monster looks like, from what colour it is to its general size and attitude.

Stats

This stat lists the monster's Fighting, Defence and Health as well as what weapons it uses and damage.

Special Rules

Any special monster characteristics, including lair details, are found here. Any special rules that apply to the monster can be found here as well.

Typical Native Climate

This will list where you are likely to find the monster and is expanded on in more detail later in the book.

Encounter Numbers

This section denotes typical encounter numbers for this monster. This is just a guide on how many of each monster you will find in a given encounter; it is not a hard and fast rule, so you can use more or less if you wish.

Treasure

Typical carried and stashed treasure will be noted here as: none, sparse, common, rich, wealthy, lair 1, lair 2 and lair 3. The treasure is generated by the games master (see Appendix).

Creature Type: This section divides monsters into one of four types: Humanoid, Monster, Undead or Animal. Humanoids are usually human-shaped; they walk upright and have arms and legs and are also usually intelligent. Monsters are weird and wonderful beasts that come in all shapes and sizes. Undead are the remains of once living people bought back from the afterlife to serve a powerful master. Animals are just that: everyday animals you could find anywhere. This category also covers giant animals.

Threat Level: A monster's threat level is an indication of how dangerous a monster is to a group of characters. A low threat level means the monster should pose no real danger. A normal threat level means the monster is challenging, but should be overcome easily enough. A high threat level means the characters will have to work hard to overcome the beast, though they should ultimately succeed. A very high threat level means it is unlikely the characters will succeed unless they are experienced. An extreme threat level is reserved for the most dangerous of monsters, and will likely kill most characters unless they are very experienced and have some powerful equipment to back them up!

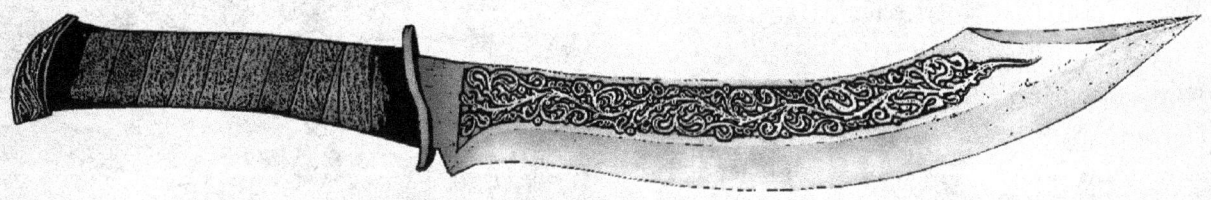

Angel

Sometimes referred to as the Warriors of Heaven, angels are divine beings in the service of the gods of good. They only rarely appear upon the world, and only in times of the greatest need. Some priests and other spiritual men and women can occasionally summon an angel to their bidding, but this happens very rarely and is only accomplished by the most devout students of the faith.

Angels appear as pale or golden skinned humans. They are very beautiful beings and radiate an aura of holy light. A set of feathery wings, usually white or golden, grow from their backs, allowing them to glide with race through the skies. When they enter battle, they wield swords imbued with holy power.

Stats: Fighting 9, Defence 17, Health 95, Damage 2-12 (2 dice)

Special Rules: The holy blade of an angel causes great damage to undead creatures and demons. An undead creature or demon hit by an angel's sword suffers double damage.

Summon Angel (Difficulty 20): Priests can learn this spell by spending 1 experience point. Successfully casting it allows the Priest to summon one angel to do his bidding for five minutes of game time. If the summons happens for an unworthy reason, the angel will turn on the summoner.

Typical Native Climate: Angels are not usually found on the Ancient World. When they are, it could be anywhere.

Encounter Numbers: 1-3 (1 dice divided by 2)

Treasure: Sparse

Creature Type: Monster

Threat Level: Extreme

Assassin

These cruel, evil, heartless individuals are nothing short of hired killers. Their whole existence revolves around finding a decent contract, hunting down and killing the victim then returning to collect their pay.

Most of these assassins started their life as orphans or abused children driven to hate by their unfortunate upbringing. By their early teens they will have been 'collected' by a guild and taught their new trade. Most assassins' guilds charge their apprentices a standard fee of 40% of any money earned to cover board, lodgings and expenses until the age of 19. Once the apprentice reaches this age they are evicted from the guild and sent on their way.

Every now and again, an assassin will become too good at their job and simply live to kill. They fall in love the adrenalin rush gained from hunting a scared victim through a secluded alley or the sheer exhilaration of watching the life drain from their unsuspecting prey.

Stats: Fighting 8, Defence 12 (plus armour), Health 15, Damage by weapon

Special Rules: The assassin can deal a deadly blow in combat. If the assassin causes maximum damage in combat, the victim must make a Strength roll (Difficulty 12) or die immediately.

Typical Native Climate: Any

Encounter Numbers: 1

Treasure: Rich or Wealthy

Creature Type: Humanoid

Threat Level: Very High

Bandit

Bandit is a generic term for outlaw, brigand, thief, cutpurse or thug. These unscrupulous people normally hang around in gangs of four or five under the rule of a gang leader or boss.

Bandits can be found just about anywhere: grave robbing old dungeons, hiding out in camps in the forest waiting to attack unsuspecting passersby and in towns or cities (normally in organised guilds). The authorities are always trying to quell these groups, though usually without much success.

Stats: Fighting 3, Defence 10 (plus armour), Health 4, Damage by weapon

Special Rules: None

Typical Native Climate: Any

Encounter Numbers: 1-6 (1 dice)

Treasure: Sparse

Creature Type: Humanoid

Threat Level: Normal

Banshee

Banshees are creatures from the spirit world who appear to foretell the deaths of mortal creatures. They appear as either a young woman, an elderly matron or a ragged old hag dressed in tattered white or grey clothing. They are often unkempt, though can sometimes appear as a beautiful girl.

Encountering a banshee is a bad sign, for they only appear when someone is about to die. They sing mournful songs of death, which can cause anyone hearing it to begin bleeding from the eyes and ears. Legend says that if a banshee is killed before she finishes her song, the person whose death she was foretelling would be spared. However, it is also said that only blessed or silver weapons can harm them.

Stats: Fighting 5, Defence 11, Health 35, Damage 2-7 (1 dice +1)

Special Rules: A banshee can only by hurt by silver or blessed weapons. In addition, anyone hearing the banshee's death song must make a Magic roll (Difficulty 12) or lose an additional 1-6 Health each combat turn (1 dice).

Typical Native Climate: Spirit world. However, they can be encountered anywhere there is life.

Encounter Numbers: 1

Treasure: None

Creature Type: Undead

Threat Level: High

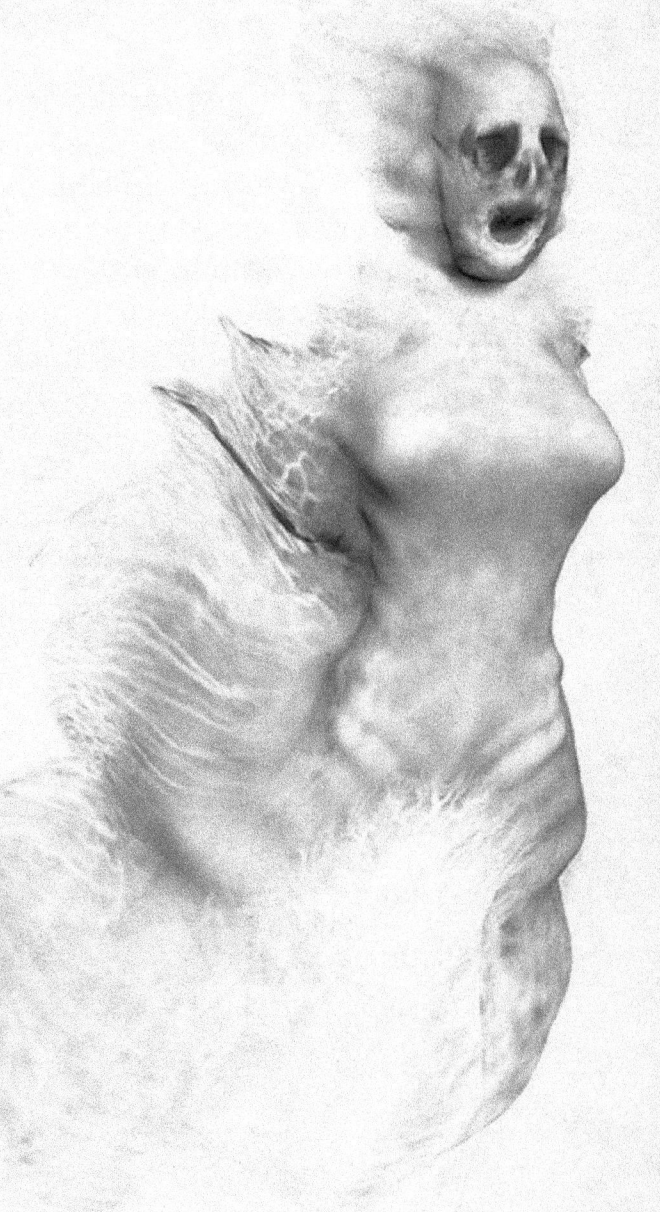

Basilisk

A basilisk is a reptilian creature that grows up to 2 metres long. They are born when a lizard or snake egg is hatched by a cockerel. The baby basilisk cracks out of its egg and devours its mother, before going on a feeding frenzy.

Basilisks look like large lizards with green-grey scales and eight legs. Their heads are very un-lizard like, resembling that of a bird instead. They are usually found in wild areas but occasionally stray close to civilization, where they are a great concern to those living there; the gaze of a basilisk is deadly, as is its venomous bite.

Stats: Fighting 3, Defence 12, Health 16, Damage 2-7 (1 dice +1)

Special Rules: Anyone damaged by a basilisk must make a Strength (Difficulty 11) check. If they fail they have fallen victim to its venom and must lose an additional 1-6 Health (roll 1 die). In addition, anyone fighting a basilisk must make sure not to meet its gaze. Unless a PC specifically closes their eyes they have a 2 in 6 chance of meeting the basilisk's gaze each turn. If this happens, they must make a Magic (Difficulty 10) check or die from the effects if it's baleful glare.

Typical Native Climate: Wilderness

Encounter Numbers: 1-2 (2-12 in lair)

Treasure: None

Creature Type: Monster

Threat Level: High

Bear

Any camping in the woods must be wary of bears. Although normally peaceful, bears can become quite vicious if provoked or if they feel threatened, rending their opponents with sharp and deadly claws. They can also wrap their powerful arms around opponents and squeeze the life out of them.

Stats: Fighting 4, Defence 11, Health 15, Damage 2-7 (1 dice +1)

Special Rules: If a bear rolls a double 6 on their Fighting roll then they inflict double damage as they hug their opponent.

Typical Native Climate: Forests and mountains

Encounter Numbers: 1-3 (1 dice divided by 2)

Treasure: None

Creature Type: Animal

Threat Level: Normal

Beastman

In ages past, mad wizards and sorcerers have often experimented with creating hybrid creatures – merging two or more creatures into an entirely new creature. Most of these experiments are complete failures but, over time, some have succeeded. The most common of these have been the beastmen.

Beastmen are basically animals that walk upright like a human. Their forms vary, from tigermen and wolfmen to snakemen and birdmen. They possess the intelligence of a human rather than that of an animal. They are usually (but not always) outcasts from society, living in scattered tribes in the deepest woods or remotest mountains. These tribes will occasionally raid small settlements in search of food, which has often led armies to seek them out to destroy them. Still, with their animal instincts and their human intelligence, the beastmen tribes survive and often prosper.

Stats: Fighting 4, Defence 11 (plus armour), Health 6, Damage by weapon or 1-6 (1 dice)

Special Rules: None

Typical Native Climate: Wilderness

Encounter Numbers: 1-6 (1 dice) or 3-18 in lair (3 dice)

Treasure: Sparse or lair 1

Creature Type: Humanoid

Threat Level: Normal

Black Knight

When one thinks of a knight, they are usually thinking of a valiant, heroic warrior clad in full armour and riding a magnificent warhorse. When mention is made of a black knight, however, people go quiet and avoid each other's gazes, for black knights are the stuff of nightmares.

A black knight is much like a normal knight, with notable exceptions. Although great warriors, they are far from valiant and heroic; instead they are rotten and evil. Instead of shining silver armour they wear armour made of black steel. Their warhorses are large and strong, though they are often feral and frothing at the mouth, and have blood red eyes.

It is believed that the black knights are an order of demon-worshipping warriors, though no one knows for sure. What is known is that when a black knight rides forth they will slay all they come across, stopping only when their mission is complete or they are killed, a task that is not easy to accomplish. One thing is for certain: those who encounter a black knight and live can think themselves blessed or very lucky.

Stats: Fighting 7, Defence 14, Health 12, Damage by weapon +1

Special Rules: The presence of a black knight can strike fear into the hearts of normal mortals. Anyone encountering a black knight must make a Charisma roll (Difficulty 11) or become afraid and suffer a -2 penalty to all dice rolls until the knight is dead or can no longer be seen.

Typical Native Climate: Any

Encounter Numbers: 1-6 (1 dice)

Treasure: Common

Creature Type: Humanoid

Threat Level: High

Boar

Boars are large, pig-like creatures with a ferocious temper. They are constantly hungry and seek out food at all times. Their aggressive temperament means that they are always a threat to travellers who stumble upon them.

Stats: Fighting 3, Defence 10, Health 7, Damage 1-6 (1 dice)

Special Rules: Boars have sharp tusks that allow them to gore their prey. Should a boar roll a double 6 on their Fighting roll in hand-to-hand combat they inflict double damage.

Typical Native Climate: Forests

Encounter Numbers: 1-3 (1 dice divided by 2)

Treasure: None

Creature Type: Animal

Threat Level: Normal

Brownie

A brownie is best described as a miniature elf. They only stand half a metre tall and are found mainly in pastoral regions or light forests. These peaceful and friendly creatures prefer to avoid combat. If threatened, they will try to negotiate a non-violent resolve before resulting to magic.

Despite their size, these creatures are extremely agile. Most have brown/rustic hair and bright blue eyes and dress in brightly coloured clothes. Brownies are master tailors and will always be found with at least a sewing kit on them. They live in large communities, which they refer to as habits, built into the ruins of old buildings or tree stumps.

On occasion, a single brownie will take a shine to a human family who live close to its habit. The brownie will sneak into the family's house in the middle of the night and perform all manner of helpful tasks: mending clothes, baking fresh bread and repairing broken tools to name a few.

Stats: Fighting 1, Defence 10, Health 2, Damage 1-3 (1 dice divided by 2)

Special Rules: Brownies are master spell casters and may cast any spell available to characters. They have an effective Magic score of 10.

Typical Native Climate: Forest

Encounter Numbers: 1-6 (1 dice) 100+ in a brownie habit

Treasure: Common

Creature Type: Humanoid

Threat Level: Low

Carnivorous Plant

In the forests and jungles of the world live many different species of plant life. Some have beneficial, medicinal qualities, while others are poisonous to all life. None are as nasty as the carnivorous plants though.

Most carnivorous plants look like a giant venus fly trap, though they can take other forms as well. They usually snare their victims by entangling them in a thick vine before dragging them towards their mouths, which are lined with vicious barb-like fangs.

Stats: Fighting 2, Defence 10, Health 27, Damage 3-8 (1 dice +2)

Special Rules: Carnivorous plants are susceptible to fire; any attacks against them that use fire cause double damage.

Typical Native Climate: Forests or jungles

Encounter Numbers: 1-3 (1 dice divided by 2)

Treasure: None

Creature Type: Monster

Threat Level: Normal

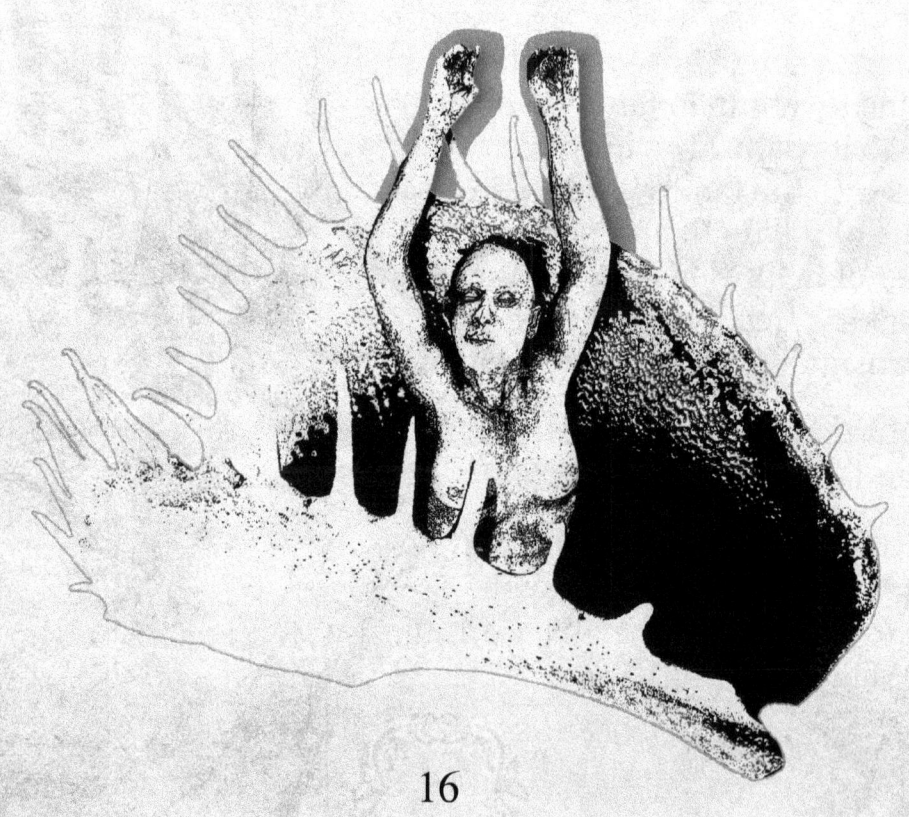

Caveman

There are few places in the world that remain untouched by time, magic and technology. Within these quiet and peaceful lands dwell Neanderthal humans, commonly known as cavemen. These people live simple lives: dwelling in caves that are heated by a makeshift campfire and hunting to survive, not for sport.

Even without magic or technology, the caveman's life is not boring (well... not to him anyway). Hunting groups go out at first light to track down hinds, bears, rabbits and any other animal that can provide both food and clothing. The females remain at the cave drying out furs and skins for clothing as well as looking after infants and preparing meat.

Stats: Fighting 3, Defence 10, Health 5, Damage by weapon (usually club or spear)

Special Rules: None

Typical Native Climate: Wilderness

Encounter Numbers: 1-6 (1 dice) in a hunting party (15-20 in small settlements)

Treasure: None to Sparse

Creature Type: Humanoid

Threat Level: Normal

Catoblepas

The catoblepas is one of the strangest looking creatures to inhabit the world. At first glance this ugly creature looks like an over-sized buffalo with a giraffe-like neck and a warthog's head. It stands on four power legs that are able to move it across land at incredible speed. Its long, powerful tail sports a bulbous, almost mace-like, end that it uses to smash its enemies and prey.

For the most part the catoblepas is herbivore, feeding on swamp reeds and tasty plants. Once a month, however, this unusual creature craves meat to round off its diet. It is during this blood lust frenzy that the adventurers are most likely to encounter it.

Stats: Fighting 8, Defence 14, Health 50, Damage 3-8 (1 dice +2)

Special Rules: The catoblepas' red eyes give host to a deadly death ray. If the player meets a catoblepas he must make a Knowledge (Difficulty 10) check to avoid the creature's gaze. If he fails this roll he stares into the eyes of the catoblepas and must make a Magic roll (Difficulty 10) or die instantly!

Typical Native Climate: Swamps

Encounter Numbers: Typically 1-2 with a single young.

Treasure: None

Creature Type: Monster

Threat Level: Very High

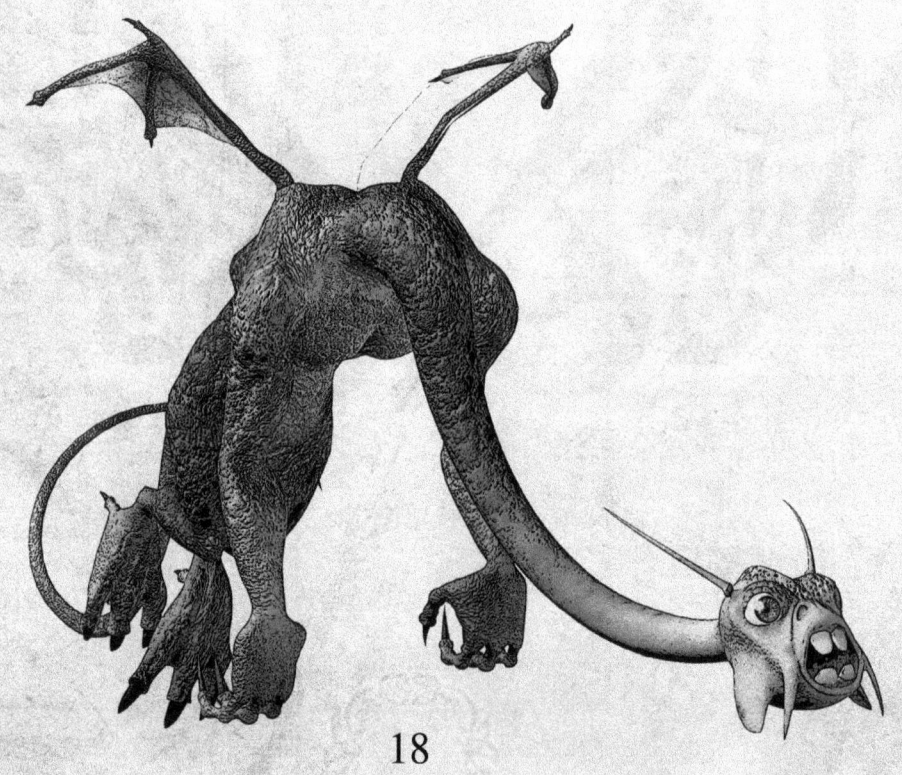

Centaur

Part human and part horse, centaurs are creatures caught between two worlds. They have the body, legs and tail of a horse, but where their necks would begin there is a human torso, arms and head. Most centaurs are nomadic creatures, wandering the plains or forests of the world with their tribes, where they hunt game. However, some centaur tribes are warlike and aggressive, raiding merchant caravans and small towns.

Stats: Fighting 4, Defence 10 (plus armour), Health 12, Damage by weapon +1 or 2-7 (1 dice +1)

Special Rules: Centaurs can speak with horses

Typical Native Climate: Forest and plains

Encounter Numbers: 1-3 (1 dice divided by 2) or 2-12 in lair (2 dice)

Treasure: Sparse to rich

Creature Type: Humanoid/Animal

Threat Level: Normal

Chimera

A chimera is a magical beast combining the parts of three different animals: a lion, a goat and a dragon. It has three heads, one of each animal type; the dragon head can breathe a gout a flame. The body is that of a large and powerful lion, with rippling muscles beneath its fur. It has the tail of a goat, which is tipped with a poisonous sting.

Often encountered in hilly areas well away from civilization, the chimera is a rare creature. Many have tried to tame this beast, but none have succeeded.

Stats: Fighting 6, Defence 16, Health 60, Damage 2-12 (2 dice).

Special Rules: The dragon head of a chimera can breathe fire at an opponent once per turn. The chimera makes a Fighting roll in addition to its normal attack; if it hits, it deals 1-6 (roll 1 die) damage to its target.

If a chimera hits with its normal attack, there is a 1 in 6 chance that it hit with the venomous tail. If this is the case, the victim must make a Strength (Difficulty 14) check. If they fail, they suffer an additional 1-6 damage (roll 1 die).

Typical Native Climate: Mainly mountains, but occasionally forests

Encounter Numbers: 1 or 1-6 (1 dice) in lair

Treasure: None with creature; Wealthy in lair

Creature Type: Monster

Threat Level: Very High

Cockatrice

Cockatrices are somewhat related to basilisks, even though they look completely different. They are born in the opposite way to the basilisk; a chicken egg is hatched by a snake or lizard. As the baby cockatrice emerges it usually kills its mother before leaving the nest in search of more prey.

A cockatrice looks like a large rooster with a snake like head and tail. Its wings are leathery instead of feathered. Those who would encounter a cockatrice would do well to remember not to get too close to its bite, for their bite can turn a man into a stone statue.

Stats: Fighting 5, Defence 11, Health 25. Damage 2-7 (1 dice +1)

Special Rules: Anyone damaged by a cockatrice must make a Magic roll (Difficulty 11). If they fail, they will be turned into a stone statue. This process is reversible, but it requires a lot of money and finding a magician or priest capable of casting the spell.

Typical Native Climate: Forest

Encounter Numbers: 1-2 or 1-6 (1 dice) in lair

Treasure: None

Creature Type: Monster

Threat Level: High

CROCODILE

Normally found in tropical, marshy areas, crocodiles can attack with blinding speed. They usually remain motionless until ready to strike, suddenly and with deadly swiftness.

Stats: Fighting 4, Defence 11, Health 12, Damage 3-8 (1 dice +2)

Special Rules: None

Typical Native Climate: Swamps

Encounter Numbers: 1-3 (1 dice divided by 2)

Treasure: None

Creature Type: Animal

Threat Level: Normal

Cyclops

These oversized humanoids are distant relatives of the giant family. They stand almost 2.5 metres tall with large, bulbous muscles growing over their often hairy grey skin. The centre of their head is dominated by a large, single red eye. Male cyclops grows a large horn from their forehead which they often use as a secondary weapon in combat. A typical cyclops will dress in an animal skin around its waist and leather bound furs on its feet.

Cyclops' are solitary creatures with no regard for anything but themselves. You won't find a cyclops attacking a heavily armed caravan, they aren't that stupid. However, it isn't uncommon for these creatures to attack single carts or lightly armed travellers. Combat tactics are not their strength. A cyclops will simply wade into combat flailing its club and head butting with its horn. If things are going bad, they are very likely to run for their lives.

Stats: Fighting 3, Defence 15, Health 50, Damage 3-8 (1 dice +2)

Special Rules: Every combat round there is a 1 in 6 chance that the cyclops will also attack with its horn. If this is the case the cyclops will get an additional attack which does 1-6 damage (1 dice).

Typical Native Climate: Any. The cyclops is a wanderer

Encounter Numbers: 1

Treasure: Common

Creature Type: Humanoid

Threat Level: High

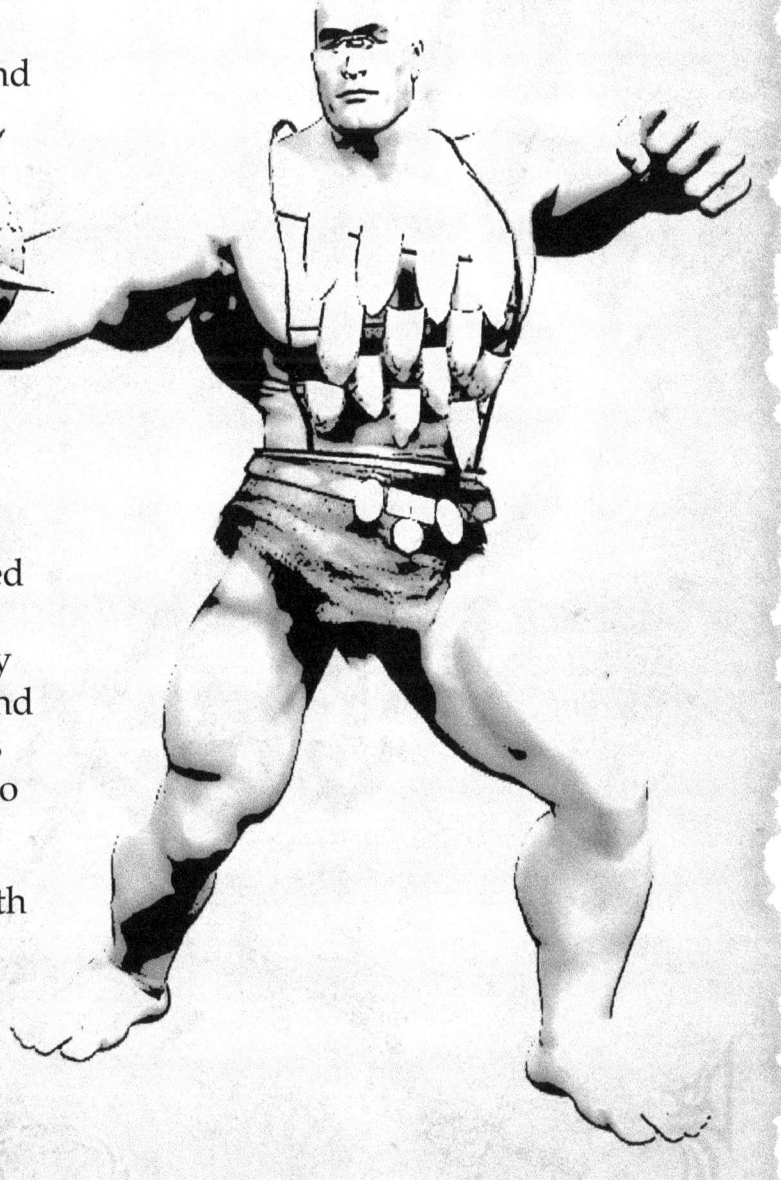

Demon

From the fiery inferno of a hellish world they come, wrecking havoc upon the world. Twisted, chaotic and purely evil, the demons are one of the greatest threats mortal life has ever known.

Although they come in many different forms, all share the same agenda: the destruction of all life. A demon can appear as a terrifying, scaly giant, or as a bloated, disease ridden abomination, or as anything in between. They are extremely aggressive; should they catch sight of even the tiniest speck of life, they will seek to destroy it.

The demons are one of the Ancient World's most feared and hated enemies, almost bringing about its destruction during an event known as the Apocalypse Storm. During this war, all life on the world banded together to stop this malevolent force, and barely succeeded, such was the strength and power of the demon hordes.

Stats: Fighting 12, Defence 18, Health 120, Damage 3-18 (3 dice)

Special Rules: Demons are terrifying monsters. Anyone seeing one must make a Charisma roll (Difficulty 14) or suffer a -2 penalty to all dice rolls until the demon is either killed or out of sight.

Summon Demon (Difficulty 22): Magicians can learn this spell by spending 1 experience point. Successfully casting it allows the magician to summon one demon to do his bidding for five minutes of game time. If the summons happens for an unworthy reason, the demon will turn on the summoner.

Typical Native Climate: Any

Encounter Numbers: 1

Treasure: None

Creature Type: Monster

Threat Level: Extreme

Doppelganger

A doppelganger is a creature that you will rarely see in its native form because it is a master of mimicry. These evil creatures will follow their intended victim to his or her place of residence (normally a wealthy person or one of some power). There they will use their ESP (extra sensory perception) ability to read the victim's mind, get to know their personality and then transform into a near perfect copy of them. Once the transformation is complete, the doppelganger will kill its victim and assume his or her identity.

In its native form the doppelganger is very plain to look at. Its body is skinny, grey skinned and completely hairless. They stand about 1.8 metres tall and, for the most part, are almost human in appearance. Doppelgangers can assume the form of any humanoid creature between the heights of 0.5 to 2 metres tall.

Stats: Fighting 4, Defence 12, Health 15, Damage 1-6 (1 dice) or by weapon

Special Rules: Doppelgangers are masters of magic with an effective magic ability of 10. They are able to cast the following spells only:

ESP (Difficulty 14): This spell gives the doppelganager the ability to read another person's mind. If the victim is aware that someone is trying to read his mind, he can make a Knowledge roll (Difficulty 12) to avoid the effects. Those unaware, the GM will secretly make a Knowledge roll (Difficulty 14) for the player. If he fails the roll the doppelganger has access to all of his victim's innermost secrets.

Transformation (Difficulty 13): This spell allows the doppelganger to transform into another humanoid. The assumed form can be either completely random (between the heights of 0.5 and 2 metres) or it can be a copy of someone the doppelganger has recently seen. If the doppelganger copies someone and then attempts to assume their life or pretend to be them for a while, there is a chance that someone close to the copied victim (a relative or close friend) may smell a rat. If the doppelganger, in his copied form, does something 'out of character' for the copied person, the relative or friend can make a Knowledge roll (Difficulty 12). If successful, they will realise a fatal flaw in the doppelganger's transformation.

Typical Native Climate: Any

Encounter Numbers: 1, normally in an assumed form

Treasure: Rich to Wealthy

Creature Type: Humanoid

Threat Level: Normal

Dragon

Powerful, mighty and terrifying; these three words and more can be used to describe the ancient race of dragons. They have four legs that end in powerful talons, and huge fang-filled mouths. Their scales are tougher than magical armour and most species can employ their huge wings in flight. These creatures are highly intelligent and most species are able to converse in many languages. There are five distinct species of dragon:

Dark Dragon: Dungeon adventurers beware, for the dark dragon could be lurking in any cavern. Their jet black scales and superb night vision make them the deadliest underground predator. Dark dragons are the smallest of the dragon kin growing to only 8 metres in length. They use their powerful claws to climb around dungeons and cavern ceilings waiting to attack.

Fire Dragon: The most common, and by far the largest, of the dragons is the fire dragon. This beast is easily recognised by its ember red scales. Its primary weapon is its ability to breathe a mighty gout of flame from its mouth. They live in mountainous areas or near volcanoes, in immense caves often dug by the dragon itself. These caves often contain a massive treasure horde gathered by the dragon over its thousand year life. Of course this leads many adventurers to attempt to slay the dragon in order to claim the treasure for themselves; sadly, but not surprisingly, most of these souls do not return.

Forest Dragon: The forest dragon is one of the smaller dragon types. An adult will normally grow to about 15 metres in length, just half the size of its fire breathing kin. These relatively good natured beasts dwell deep within the heart of large forests and woods. Their scales range in colour from dark green to rustic brown depending on the climate of their surroundings. As you expect from a creature like this, the forest dragon is equipped with huge talons and teeth. These instruments, however, are mainly used for scaling tall trees. These dragons live in caves that have been dug into the roots of the largest trees in the forest.

Ice Dragon: Far in the distant north where glaciers and raging snow storms are common place you will find the dreaded ice dragon. These dragons do not have wings like their other kin, but they do have huge oversized front talons to help them traverse the ice and snow. Despite their large bodies (adults grow to 20m in length) these creatures are cunning predators. They hide amongst snow dunes waiting for a tasty meal (normally polar bears or large walrus). They strike with lightning speed and accuracy using their talons to rend their prey. Ice Dragons can only communicate in their own language and cannot cast spells.

Lightning Dragon: Lightning dragons live up to their name in every sense of the word: their brilliant blue scales shine like an electric storm; they can fly faster than any other dragon and they can launch a devastating lightning bolt from their mouth. Unlike their fellow dragon kin the lightning dragon prefers to move about and fight on its hind legs. The lightning dragon will grow to over 20m in length and can communicate in a variety of languages including the human tongue.

Stats: Fighting 16, Defence 20, Health 100, Damage 3-18 (3 dice)

Special Rules: All dragons have a breath weapon that they may use in combat. The effects of this weapon vary depending on the dragon species, as listed below. Each dragon may have additional special rules, which are also listed below.

Dark Dragon: Once every three turns a dark Dragon can breathe a cloud of paralysing gas; they can do this even if they attack. The dragon makes a Fighting roll and, if it hits, the victim must make a Strength roll (Difficulty 11). If he fails the roll he cannot move for 5 game minutes.

Fire Dragon: Once every three turns a fire dragon can breathe fire at an opponent; they can do this even if they attack. The dragon makes a Fighting roll and, if it hits, inflicts 2-12 damage upon the victim (roll 2 dice).

Fire dragons are immune to any damage inflicted by fire.

Fire dragons are also accomplished spell casters and may cast any spell available to characters. They have an effective Magic score of 9.

Forest Dragon: Once every three turns a forest dragon can breathe a toxic gas at an opponent; they can do this even if they attack. The dragon makes a Fighting roll and, if it hits, inflicts 1-6 damage upon the victim.

Forest dragons hate fire and will avoid it wherever possible.

Forest dragons have limited magic ability (effective Magic score of 4) and can cast the following spell only.

Tangle roots (Difficulty 11): Weeds, roots and branches wrap themselves around a single target. The target must make a Strength roll (Difficulty 10) or suffer a -2 penalty to Defence for 5 minutes of game time.

Ice Dragon: Once every three turns an ice dragon can breathe a blast of cold air at an opponent; they can do this even if they attack. The dragon makes a Fighting roll and, if it hits, inflicts 1-6 damage upon the victim.

Ice dragons are immune to any damage inflicted by cold/ice.

Lightning Dragon: Once every three turns a lightning dragon can omit a devastating lightning bolt at an opponent; they can do this even if they attack. The dragon makes a Fighting roll and, if it hits, inflicts 2-12 damage upon the victim.

Lightning dragons are immune to any damage inflicted by electricity.

Lightning dragons, like the fire dragon, are also accomplished spell casters and may cast any spell available to characters. They have an effective Magic score of 8.

Typical Native Climate: Dungeons (dark dragons); mountains or volcanoes (fire dragon); forest or jungle (forest dragon); tundra (ice dragon); or any (lightning dragon).

Encounter Numbers: 1

Treasure: Lair 1-3

Creature Type: Monster

Threat Level: Extreme

Dragonman

Like beastmen, the creatures known as dragonmen are an amalgamation of two creatures, in this case dragon and humanoid. Unlike beastmen, however, dragonmen are much more powerful. Created by sorcery, dragonmen stand over two metres tall. They possess scaly skin, coloured a dark greenish colour, and sprout large wings from their backs that allow them to fly. They are powerful and dangerous enemies.

Dragonmen are shunned by both other humanoids for their war-like nature, as well as dragons, who see them as an unnatural creation. For their part, the dragonmen are more than happy to be separate from both groups, living their lives in isolated tribes throughout the mountains and remote areas of the world.

Stats: Fighting 6, Defence 13, Health 10, Damage 3-8 (1 dice +2)

Special Rules: None

Typical Native Climate: Wilderness

Encounter Numbers: 1-6 (1 dice) or 3-18 (3 dice) in lair

Treasure: Sparse or lair 1

Creature Type: Humanoid

Threat Level: High

Dryad

Dryads are extremely beautiful and highly intelligent tree spirits. Legend says that these mystical creatures are reincarnated spirits of some of the oldest trees in the forests, but this is just hear say. However, dryads are mystically bound to a single tree. They spend their lives tending, nurturing and keeping the tree from harm. They cannot travel more than 50 metres from their bound tree or they will cease to exist.

These creatures are very kind and timid and are only seen if they want to be seen. Standing about the same height as an elf, dryads are the epitome of beauty. They normally wear only a single, almost see through, item of clothing (normally a long white dress) and like to run about the forests barefoot.

Due to their kind nature, the dryad is not at all violent. They never carry a weapon of any description, only small tools that are used to tend their tree. If threatened, or their tree is threatened, they will use a very powerful beguile spell to charm their enemy.

Stats: Fighting 1, Defence 10, Health 4, Damage 1 point

Special Rules: Dryads can cast a single spell with an effective Magic score of 10. They are able to cast the following spell only:

Beguile (Difficulty 13): When cast on a humanoid creature the victim will become the dryad's best friend. The victim will do whatever the dryad asks, as long as it doesn't involve the victim committing suicide or causing some other harm to themselves. The beguiled victim will even attack his own party members if he thinks they are a threat to his new best friend. The victim may make a Charisma roll (Difficulty 14) to avoid the effects.

Typical Native Climate: Forests

Encounter Numbers: 1

Treasure: None to sparse

Creature Type: Monster

Threat Level: Low

Dwarf

A dwarf is a short, human-like being. They stand roughly a metre tall, but are stocky and broad-shouldered. They prefer to live underground rather than on the surface, where they mine the earth for gems and precious metals, two items they greatly treasure. In their underground tunnels and mines, which are expertly made, they pass the time crafting fine weapons and armour, or drinking ale and telling stories of their ancestors. This, of course, is if they are not fighting off hordes of goblins or other monsters, who frequently invade their underground strongholds.

Stats: Fighting 4, Defence 10 (plus armour), Health 6, Damage by weapon

Special Rules: Dwarfs can see in the dark without need for a source of light. They gain a +1 bonus to their Fighting score in combat against goblins.

Typical Native Climate: Underground mostly, but can be anywhere.

Encounter Numbers: 1-6 (1 dice); hundreds in towns or cities

Treasure: Sparse to Wealthy

Creature Type: Humanoid

Threat Level: Normal

Eagle

Eagles make their nests in the hills and mountains of the world. Occasionally they will fly down to lower regions to hunt. Eagle eggs are prized by collectors and traders,

Stats: Fighting 3, Defence 10, Health 6, Damage 1-6 (1 dice)

Special Rules: None

Typical Native Climate: Mountains

Encounter Numbers: 1

Treasure: None

Creature Type: Animal

Threat Level: Normal

Elemental

An elemental is a spirit-being that occupies a body made out of one of the four elements: air, earth, fire or water. They originate from the spirit worlds and can only walk on the mortal world when either summoned by a powerful magician or when they enter through a spirit gate. If the body that the elemental is occupying is destroyed on the mortal world, it will return to the spirit world.

If summoned, the elemental is at the complete control of the magician. If encountered as a creature that has passed through a spirit gate, it will attack any humanoids on sight.

Each of the four different types of elemental appears in a different manner, depending on its element type.

Air Elementals: An air elemental can only be summoned into an area where there is a high wind. This elemental is almost invisible when encountered out in the open; however it will show itself to the magician that summoned it as a large shifting cloud.

In combat, the air elemental can create a concentrated gust of wind that will strike its enemy like a hammer.

Earth Elementals: This is the most common of the elementals. It can be summoned anywhere that there is natural stone, precious stones or metals or any type of soil. The earth elemental will mould the earth around it into a huge humanoid bulk with a blank, almost expressionless face. This elemental has no special powers like its kin, other than its sheer brute strength.

Fire Elementals: The fire elemental can only be summoned into fire no smaller than 2 metres across by 1 metre high. This elemental is the fiercest of them all but it is also limited in movement. A fire elemental cannot pass over water or any material that is not flammable. This can severely limit the elemental in combat.

A fire elemental's form on the Ancient World is that of a huge, blue flamed fire. It has two appendages that resemble arms of a sort, which it uses to attack with, and two piercing yellow eyes.

Water Elementals: Water elementals can only be summoned into a body of water that is a minimum of 2 metres deep by 4 metres wide. They can only move in water (fresh or sea) and cannot travel or move on dry land. When summoned they resemble a huge stationary wave with two algae-green eyes that bob in and out of the water. It attacks by using its large watery arms to smash its opponents.

Water elementals are particularly dangerous to small ships. They can easily capsize a small vessel of up to 3 tonnes in weight. Some evil magicians use their summoned water elementals to control shipping lanes or sink cargo ships. The elementals then collect up the cargo and drag it to the beach where the magician can then take it to his castle or stronghold.

Stats: Fighting 8, Defence 12, Health 75, Damage 2-12 (2 dice)

Special Rules: Elementals can be summoned by a magician of sufficient power. Any magician may learn the following spell by spending 1 experience point.

Summon Elemental (Difficulty 18): This spell will summon an elemental of the magicians choosing to serve him. The summoned creature will stay 100% faithful to its master for the duration of the spell which is 1 hour or if the elemental is slain.

Each of the different elemental types also it has its own special rules.

Air Elementals: Once every 3 combat rounds the air elemental can turn into a huge tornado. Anyone within 10 metres of this vortex must make a Strength roll (Difficulty 14) or take an extra 2-12 points of damage.

Earth Elementals: Being made of dirt and stone, earth elementals are tough. They have a Defence score of 16 rather than 12.

Fire Elementals: Once every 3 combat rounds a fire elemental can cast Enhanced Fiery Blast. The creature has an effective Magic score of 10

Enhanced Fiery Blast (Difficulty 16): Choose one enemy. A bolt of flame shoots from your palm and hits it in the chest. The target suffers 2-12 damage (roll 2 dice).

Water Elementals: Because water elementals are invisible in water they can surprise their victims. During the first round of combat, if the elemental has not revealed itself to the players they will suffer -3 Defence.

Typical Native Climate: Any or water only (water elementals)

Encounter Numbers: 1

Treasure: None

Creature Type: Monster

Threat Level: Very High

Elf

Elves are a race of angelic, human-like beings. Although growing to about the same height as a human, elves are much more slender and graceful as well as more beautiful. Their skin is pale in colour and their eyes bright; their ears are pointed rather than round.

Elves make their homes in woodland areas where they live extremely long lives. They are creatures of magic and casting spells comes naturally to them. They tend to avoid other races as much as they can, preferring to avoid the troubles of the world.

Stats: Fighting 3, Defence 10, Health 4, Damage by weapon

Special Rules: Elves are able to cast the following spells: Levitation, Mage Light, Protective Aura and Healing Hands. They have a Magic score of 6.

Typical Native Climate: Forest

Encounter Numbers: 1-6 (1 dice) or hundreds in settlements

Treasure: Sparse to rich

Creature Type: Humanoid

Threat Level: Normal

Gargoyle

Gargoyles were originally invented as masonry sculptures designed to direct rain water away from buildings by channelling it through a wide opening in its mouth. Many years ago, a magician thought that these creatures would make excellent lookouts for his tower. He brought a pair to life and ordered them to watch over his tower while he went gathering potion components from a nearby forest. When he returned, the pair of gargoyles had fled. This original pair is responsible for the gargoyle population of the Ancient World.

A gargoyle stands about 1 metre tall with rough, grey coloured skin and a pair of large leather wings. They like to sit in a hunched position and can stay so still that they actually look like statues. On their hind legs they have huge talons that they use for raking their enemies from the air. Gargoyles tend to stay together in family groups and prefer to nest in dark caves.

Stats: Fighting 5, Defence 11, Health 10, Damage 2-7 (1dice +1)

Special Rules: none

Typical Native Climate: Forests and mountains

Encounter Numbers: 1-6 (1 dice) or 10+ in their cave lair

Treasure: None

Creature Type: Monster

Threat Level: Normal

Genie

Genies originate from the same spirit worlds as the elementals. It is extremely rare to find one on the mortal world that hasn't been summoned and bound by a powerful magician. Typically a genie is bound to a single item such as a ring, vase or lamp where it will reside until it has fulfilled its master's wishes.

Coming from the spirit world, the genie is almost a magic using air elemental. They appear as the top half of a human male or female (normally dark skinned and muscular) that turns to wispy, smoky air from their waists to their feet. As with most summoned creatures, the genie remains faithful to its master while bound.

A genie's time in binding can be very short to many years in service, depending on the magician that summoned it. By way of bowing to the power of the magician, the genie promises to perform 3 tasks (within its own power). Once these three tasks are complete the genie is returned to the spirit world.

Stats: Fighting 7, Defence 13, Health 60, Damage 1-6 (1 dice)

Special Rules: Genies are amongst the most powerful magicians to walk on Hammerax. They have access to any spell found in both this book and The QUERP Rulebook (with the exception of Summon and Bind Genie) and have an effective Magic score of 15.

The following spell may be learnt my magicians by spending 1 experience point.

Summon & Bind Genie (Difficulty 18): This spell will summon a genie to serve the magician. The summoned genie will stay 100% faithful to the caster until it has performed 3 tasks or it is destroyed. The binding item must be made of either gold or silver with a value of at least 500 gold coins. If the caster of the spell is killed before the genie has performed its 3 tasks it will remain in the binding vessel (ring, lamp etc.). It will then serve the next person to find it so that it can return to the spirit world.

Typical Native Climate: Any

Encounter Numbers: 1

Treasure: None

Creature Type: Monster

Threat Level: Very High

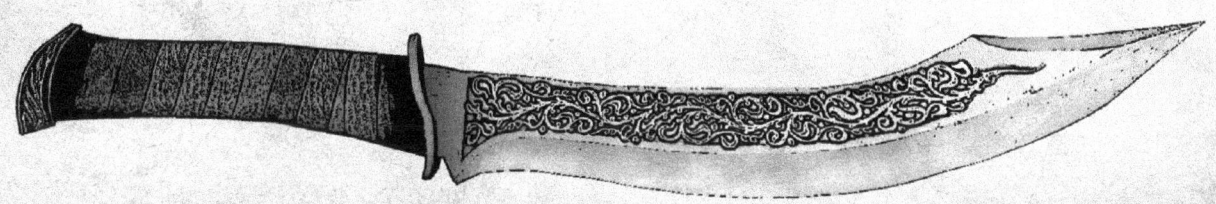

Ghoul

Ghouls were once a race of humans who became cannibalistic, eating their own kind in the belief that this would grant them immortal life. Outcast from their own society, they became of race of degenerate wanderers, emaciated and filthy. Their belief of immortal life was not a flase one as, through their practices and rituals, they became undead creatures, no longer truly human.

Ghouls today are often found amongst other humans, though never openly, as their appearance would give them away immediately. Instead they skulk in the shadows, often amongst graveyards, waiting for some warm flesh to feed upon.

Stats: Fighting 3, Defence 11, Health 4, Damage 1-6 (1 dice)

Special Rules: None

Typical Native Climate: Urban

Encounter Numbers: 1-6 (1 dice) or 3-18 in lair (3 dice)

Treasure: None or wealth in lair

Creature Type: Undead

Threat Level: Normal

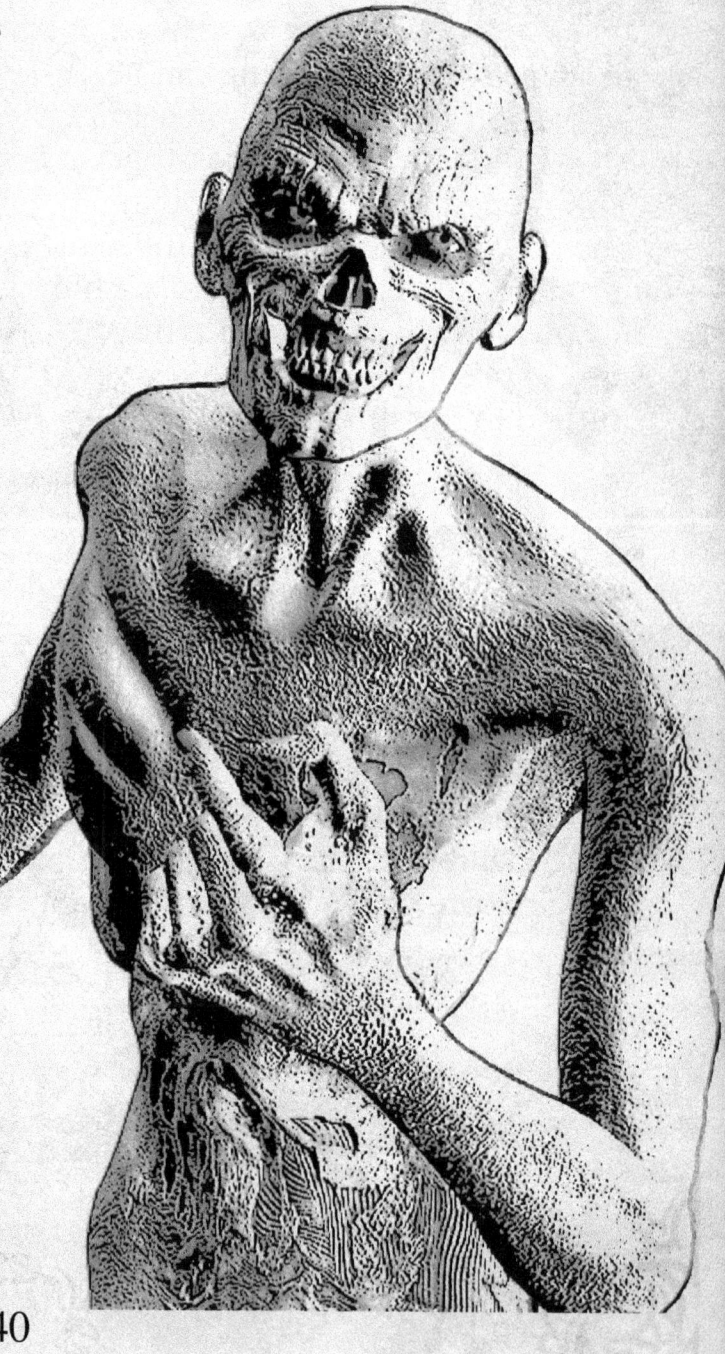

Giant

Giants are tall human-like creatures. In nearly all respects they look like a human male or female; the only difference being that they grow up to 4 metres tall. They are slow-witted and easily tricked by cunning adventurers.

Giants live amongst the hills and mountains of the world, where they pass the time hunting and building mighty homes.

Stats: Fighting 4, Defence 16, Health 65, Damage 2-12 (2 dice)

Special Rules: None

Typical Native Climate: Mountains

Encounter Numbers: 1 (3-5 in small family groups)

Treasure: Common to Rich (Lair 1 in family groups)

Creature Type: Humanoid

Threat Level: Very high

Giant Bat

Giant bats are about twice the size of their regular cousins. They hide in the shadows and attack in a flurry of fangs and wings.

Stats: Fighting 2, Defence 10, Health 1, Damage 1-5 (1 dice -1)

Special Rules: Giant bats gain a +2 bonus to their initiative rolls.

Typical Native Climate: Dungeons

Encounter Numbers: 2-12 (2 dice)

Treasure: None

Creature Type: Animal

Threat Level: Low

Giant Centipede

Growing up to a metre long, giant centipedes have fierce teeth and tough skin. While they normally avoid other creatures, preferring to feed on the carcases of the dead, they will attack if hungry enough.

Stats: Fighting 4, Defence 10, Health 2, Damage 1-4 (1 dice -2)

Special Rules: The bite of a giant centipede is venomous. Anyone damaged by one must make a Strength roll (Difficulty 11) or lose an additional 1-6 (1 dice) Health.

Typical Native Climate: Dungeons, urban or forests

Encounter Numbers: 1-6 (1 dice)

Treasure: None

Creature Type: Animal

Threat Level: Normal

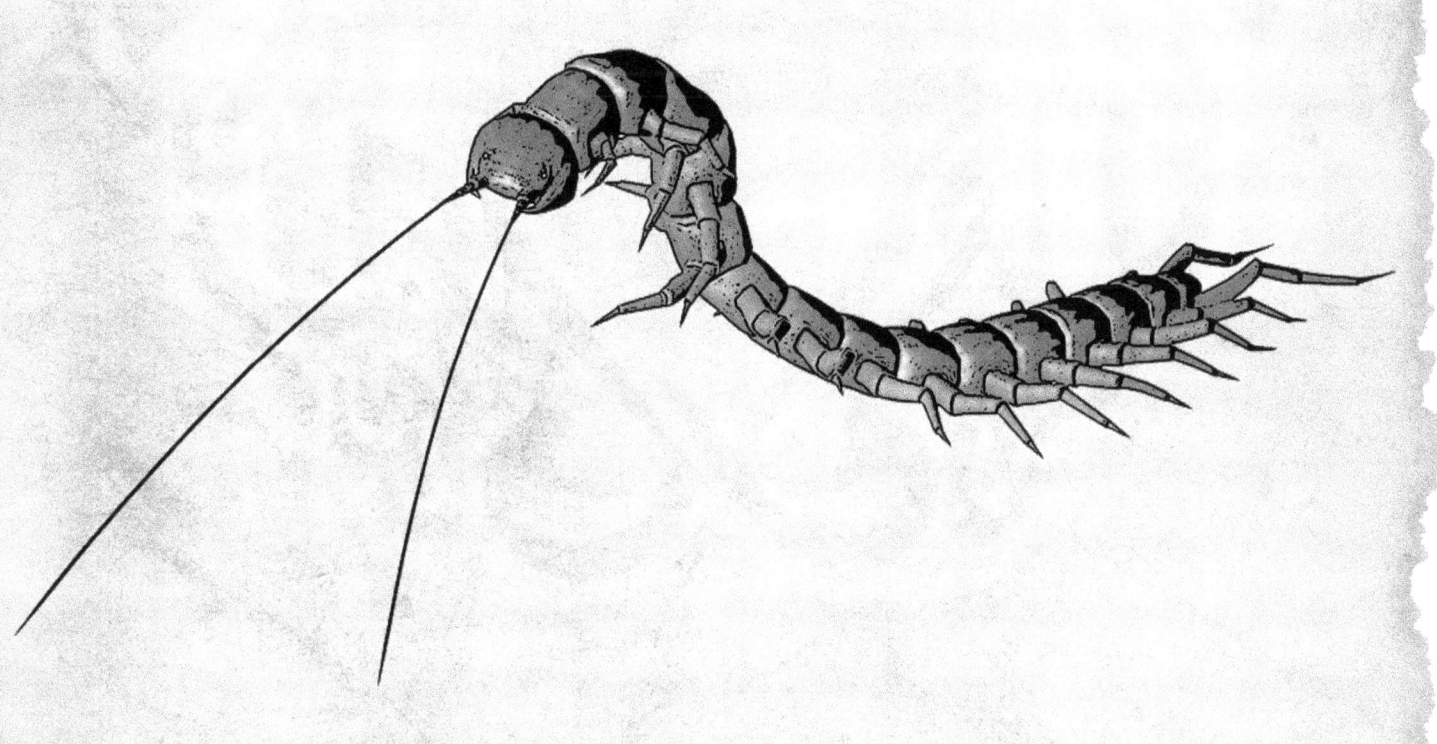

Giant Eagle

Making their homes amongst the tallest peaks of the world, giant eagles are a rare and beautiful sight. These majestic beasts grow up to 3 metres tall and have wingspans of almost 7 metres. They are intelligent and wise, and serve the forces of good in their fight against evil.

Giant eagles have been known to ally themselves with elves on regular occasions, and less frequently with humans. They will allow elves to ride them, even into battle where they make fearsome opponents.

Stats: Fighting 6, Defence 11, Health 15, Damage 3-8 (1 dice +2)

Special Rules: None

Typical Native Climate: Mountains

Encounter Numbers: 1

Treasure: None

Creature Type: Animal

Threat Level: High

Giant Rat

These vermin often grow to the size of a dog and sometimes larger. They infest sewers, dungeons and other dark, dank places. They often carry disease as well.

Stats: Fighting 2, Defence 10, Health 2, Damage 1-6 (1 dice)

Special Rules: After combat, anyone damaged by a giant rat must make a Strength roll (Difficulty 10). If they fail they have contracted a disease and must deduct -1 from all dice rolls until cured, or until three days of game time have passed.

Typical Native Climate: Dungeons and urban

Encounter Numbers: 2-12 (2 dice)

Treasure: None

Creature Type: Animal

Threat Level: Low

Giant Scorpion

The desert sands hide many dangers, not least of which are the massive bodies of giant scorpions. Growing to about the size of a horse, these creatures hide under the sand awaiting their prey, before scuttling forward to attack. Although their two great pincers are dangerous, one must also look out for the venomous sting in their tail.

Stats: Fighting 4, Defence 13, Health 20, Damage 3-8 (1 dice +2)

Special Rules: Whenever a giant scorpion attacks, roll a dice. On a 1, it attacks with its sting, which deals 2-12 damage (2 dice). In addition, anyone struck by the sting must make a Strength roll (Difficulty 11) or lose an additional 1-6 (1 dice) Health.

Typical Native ZClimate: Desert

Encounter Numbers: 1-3 (1 dice divided by 2)

Treasure: None

Creature Type: Animal

Threat Level: High

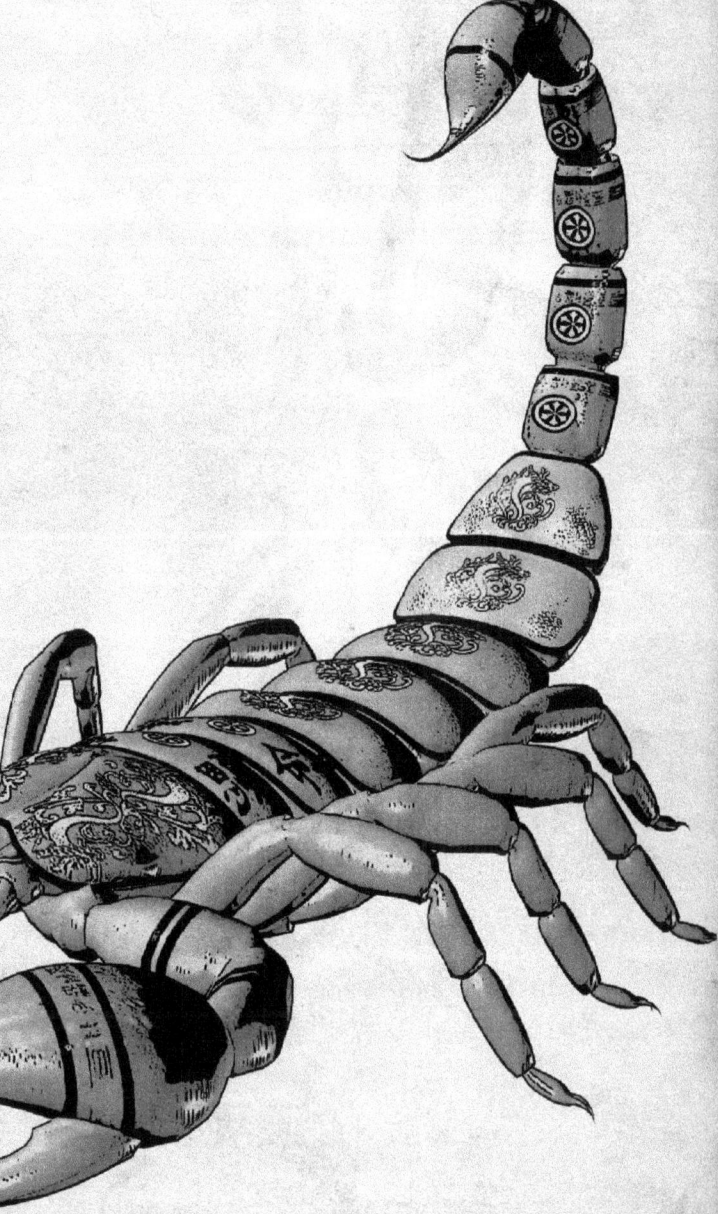

Giant Snake

Giant snakes are larger versions of their cousins, often growing up to five metres in length. They are venomous and dangerous, with sharp fangs that can pierce a man's chest.

Stats: Fighting 5, Defence 11, Health 18, Damage 2-7 (1 dice +1)

Special Rules: The bite of a giant snake is venomous. Anyone damaged by one must make a Strength roll (Difficulty 12) or lose an additional 1-6 (1 dice) Health.

Typical Native Climate: Wilderness

Encounter Numbers: 1-6 (1 dice)

Treasure: None

Creature Type: Animal

Threat Level: High

Giant Spider

Giant spiders are just that: enormous spiders that have grown much larger than their smaller, normal counterparts. They live underground or in dark, dense woodlands, where they spin strong sticky webs to trap their victims. Once trapped, the spider moves in slowly, savouring the fear of their victims as they prepare to be injected with the spider's deadly venom. Only if they are hungry or threatened first will they attack prey not caught in their webs.

Some goblins have been known to have success in taming giant spiders, using them to ride into battle.

Stats: Fighting 4, Defence 11, Health 20, Damage 1-6 (1 dice)

Special Rules: Anyone damaged by a giant spider must make a Strength roll at Difficulty 12. If they fail, they lose a further 1-6 Health (roll 1 die).

If a creature becomes caught in a giant spider's web, they must pass a Strength roll at Difficulty 12 in order to break free from it.

Typical Native Climate: Dungeons or forests

Encounter Numbers: 1-3 (1 dice divided by 2)

Treasure: None

Creature Type: Animal

Threat Level: High

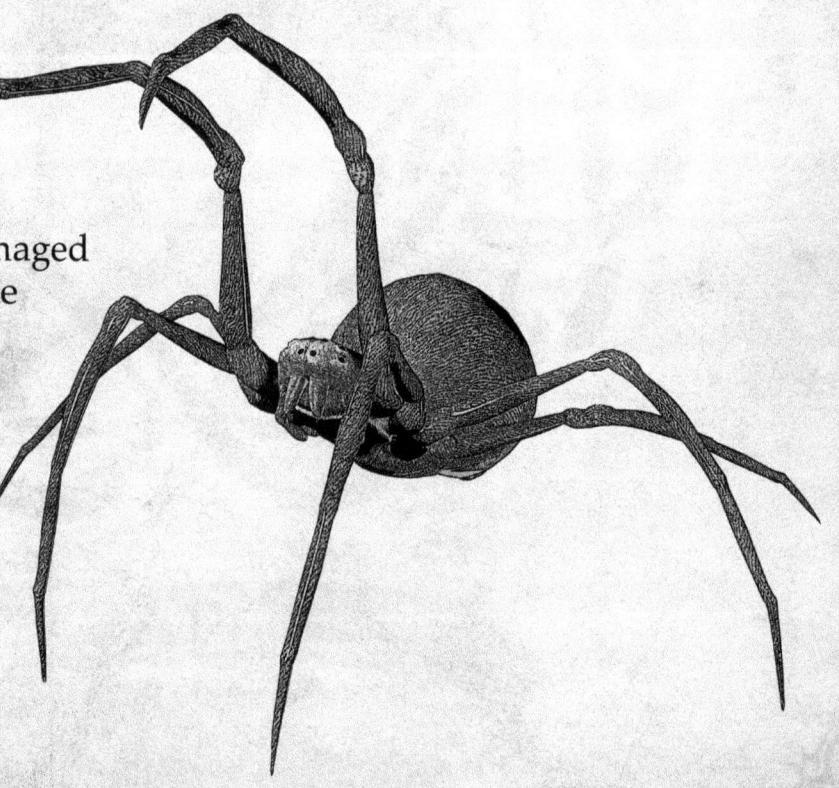

Giant Wolf

Giant wolves are much like their smaller relatives; they hunt in packs, picking on smaller and weaker creatures. However they are much bigger, often as large as a small pony.

Stats: Fighting 4, Defence 10, Health 6, Damage 2-7 (1 dice +1)

Special Rules: If two or more giant wolves are facing the same opponent in hand-to-hand combat, all of those wolves gain +1 Fighting.

Typical Native Climate: Forests and mountains

Encounter Numbers: 2-12 (2 dice)

Treasure: None

Creature Type: Animal

Threat Level: Normal

Gnome

Gnomes are a diminutive race of human-like beings. They closely resemble dwarfs in appearance, though they are shorter and not quite as stocky.

Gnomes live in small societies, usually around a series of low rolling hills. The gnomes make their homes within the hills themselves, burrowing out small abodes beneath the ground. These are small and functional and usually very cosy. The outsides of the hills are often made up of elaborate and beautiful gardens, as gnomes love nothing more than gardening.

Stats: Fighting 4, Defence 10, Health 4, Damage by weapon

Special Rules: Gnomes can speak the language of animals.

Typical Native Climate: Forests

Encounter Numbers: 1-6 (50+ in a small society)

Treasure: Common to Rich

Creature Type: Humanoid

Threat Level: Normal

Goblin

A goblin is a short, humanoid creature about a metre tall. They are twisted and stunted, with green-brown, warty skin. They live underground where they infest natural and dwarf-made tunnels like rats. This often leads them into conflict with the dwarven people, between which an ancient hatred exists. In fact, it is often said that goblins were once dwarfs corrupted by foul, evil magic. Of course, the dwarfs vehemently dispute this.

Goblins can sometimes be found above ground. Usually they come out at night, where they sneak into homes and barns in search of things to steal.

Stats: Fighting 2, Defence 10, Health 3, Damage by weapon

Special Rules: None

Typical Native Climate: Dungeons

Encounter Numbers: 1-6 (50+ in dungeon lairs)

Treasure: None to common (rich in lair)

Creature Type: Humanoid

Threat Level: Low

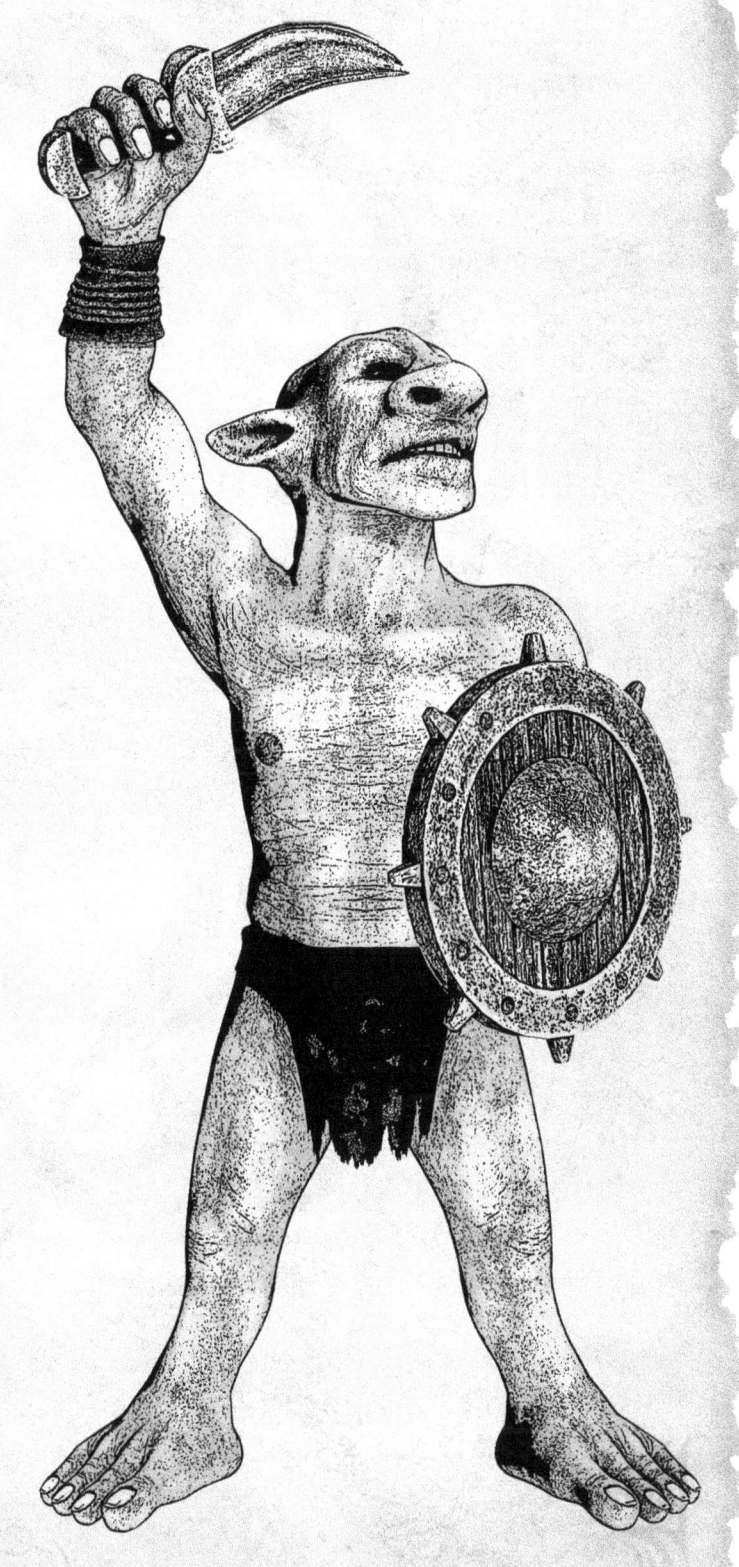

Golem

A golem is, in a short description, an animated statue that has been made and brought to life by a magician. The magician can create the golem from a variety of materials including stone, clay, wood or iron. The process is an arduous task that takes many weeks to perform; however, the results are worth it. The magician begins the process by finding (or buying) a large, single piece of his chosen golem material. The material must be a single piece or the spell will not work. If he has any artistic ability he will begin to sculpt the chosen material into a bipedal form. If he has no artistic ability he will have to find someone to create the sculpture for him, adding to the expense.

Once the sculpture is complete, a process that can take many weeks, the magician will begin the spell to bind an entity from the spirit worlds to his creation. This process alone can take quite some time as the spirit must be willing. When the binding is complete the golem is 100% under the control of the magician and will do whatever he commands. A common task for these creations is to guard special rooms for the magician, normally treasure rooms.

Stats: Fighting 5, Defence 15, Health 25, Damage 2-7 (1 dice +1)

Special Rules: Golems can only be created by means of a magical spell. Magicians may learn this spell by spending 1 experience point.

Create & Bind Golem (Difficulty 16): This spell will give artificial life to the magician's golem. The golem will stay 100% faithful to its master for the duration of its life. The requisite for this spell is a bipedal statue standing 1.5 to 2.5 metres tall made from a single piece of clay, stone, wood or iron.

Typical Native Climate: Any

Encounter Numbers: 1

Treasure: None

Creature Type: Monster

Threat Level: High

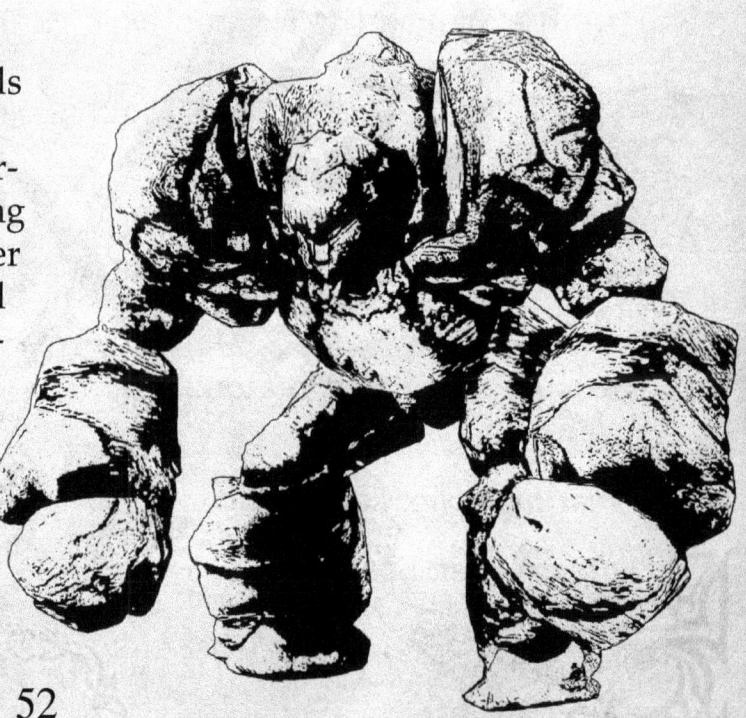

Gorgon

Gorgons are ferocious, snake-like creatures that dwell deep within dark caverns. They have the basic appearance of a human female, with some notable exceptions. Their eyes glow bright red even in the brightest lights. Their skin is covered in fine scales that will deflect even the sharpest of blades and where their hair would be is instead a nest of writhing snakes. The gorgon is malicious and evil and because of this it will attack just about anything and everything on sight. Its touch is poisonous, and can turn a man to stone.

Stats: Fighting 2, Defence 10, Health 35, Damage 1-6 (1 dice)

Special Rules: Anyone suffering damage from a gorgon must make a Strength roll (Difficulty 12) or be turned to stone. The only way to undo this is by killing the gorgon.

Typical Native Climate: Dungeons

Encounter Numbers: 1-3 (1 dice divided by 2)

Treasure: None. The skin of the gorgon can be used to create magical plate armour.

Creature Type: Humanoid

Threat Level: High

Gorilla

The gorillas of the jungles of the world are powerful creatures, standing much taller than a normal man. They attack their opponents with their great fists, pounding them into the ground until all that remains is a broken body.

Stats: Fighting 4, Defence 11, Health 18, Damage 3-8 (1 dice +2)

Special Rules: None

Typical Native Climate: Jungle

Encounter Numbers: 1-6 (1 dice)

Treasure: None

Creature Type: Animal

Threat Level: Normal

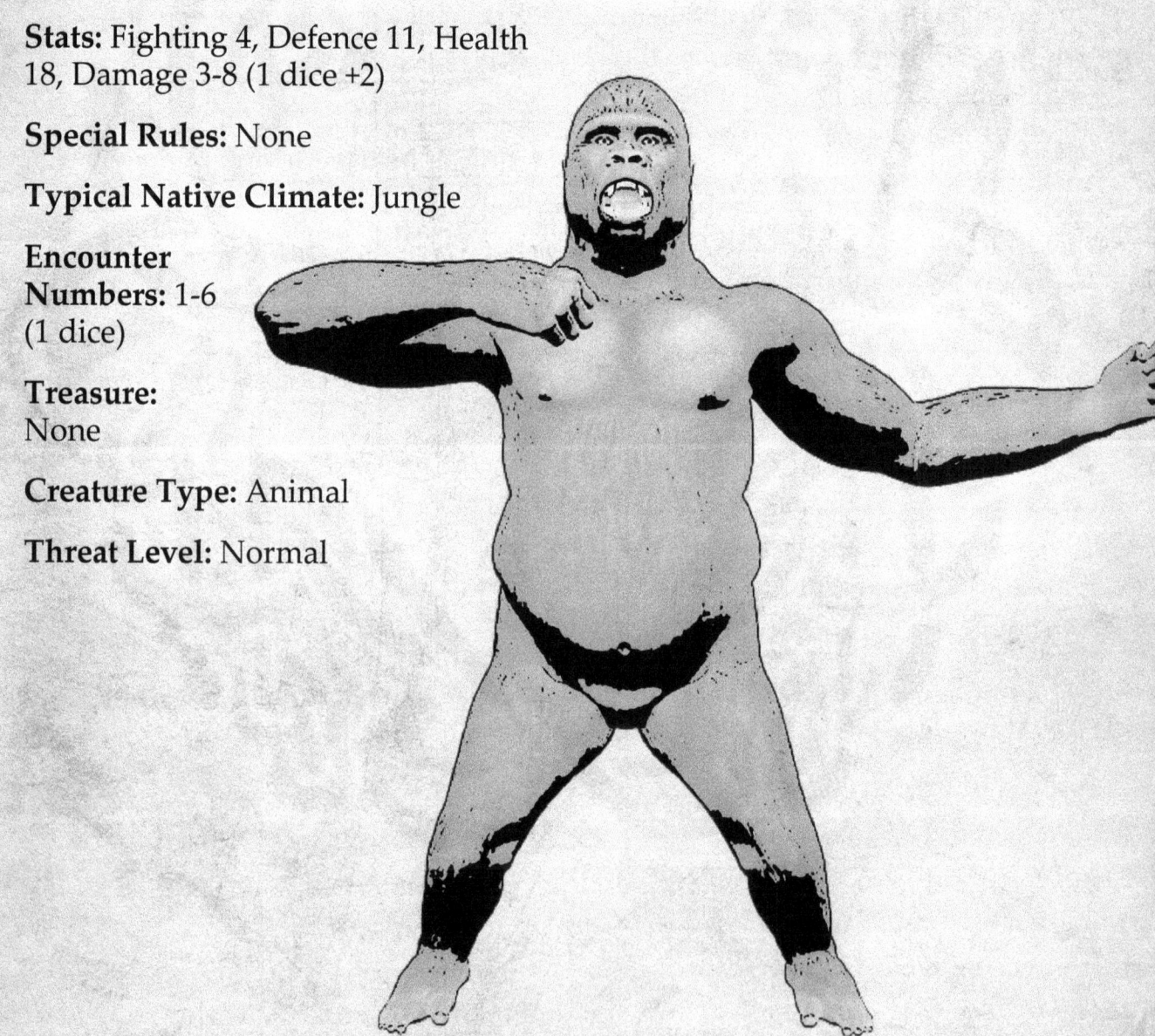

Griffon

The griffon is a mystical beast with the fore half of an eagle and the hind half of a lion. It stands about 1.5 metres tall with golden brown fur and feathers on its wings. Its favourite meal is horse meat. They have been known to snatch a rider's mount from under them, sending the rider plummeting to the ground.

These creatures are the ultimate predator, being equipped with a razor sharp beak, huge deadly talons on their front legs and large claws for raking on their rear paws. They travel in packs, similar to their lion cousins, and live in huge nests like their eagle cousins. If reared from a young cub, a griffon will make a loyal mount and a good friend.

Stats: Fighting 8, Defence 12, Health 50, Damage 2-12 (2 dice)

Special Rules: The griffon can fly and, if trained, carry a single rider.

Typical Native Climate: Mountains

Encounter Numbers: 2-12 (2 dice)

Treasure: None (Wealthy in their nests)

Creature Type: Monster

Threat Level: Very High

Harpy

Harpies are evil, wicked avian creatures that like to taunt and eat humans and their kin. Their bodies have the lower half and wings of a vulture while their upper half is that of a young, but unkempt, woman. A horrible smelling odour surrounds the harpy and everything it touches. Their clothes are normally old rags and old pieces of jewellery.

The sweet singing voice of the harpy has the ability to charm all humanoids. They sit in high trees overlooking trade routes through woodlands and forests waiting for hunters, traders and general passersby. When a victim is near they start to sing. Their voice charms the human into an almost trance-like state. They cannot do anything but sit and listen to the harpy sing. Once the harpy has its captive audience it jumps on its victim, raking them with its sharp claws and teeth.

Stats: Fighting 4, Defence 11, Health 16, Damage 2-7 (1 dice +1)

Special Rules: Harpies singing voices have a spell-like charming effect on humanoids and because of this they have an effective Magic score of 9.

Harpies Song (Difficulty 12): The voice of the harpy has a very good chance of charming any humanoid that is within hearing distance. The victim must make a Charisma roll (Difficulty 12) or become transfixed to the harpy and be unable to move or take any other actions. This effect only lasts while the harpy is singing. The effect can be broken by covering the ears of the victim or when the harpy stops singing.

Typical Native Climate: Wilderness

Encounter Numbers: 1-6 (1 dice)

Treasure: None to rich

Creature Type: Monster

Threat Level: High

Hell Hound

This canine is bred from the very fires of hell itself. It stands almost a metre tall at the shoulder and has ember coloured fur. Its eyes glow an evil red that can be seen just as well in the daytime as they can at night. Their breath is so hot that flames drip from their jowls.

Typical Native Climate: Dungeons

Encounter Numbers: Pack 2-7 (1 dice +1)

Treasure: None

Creature Type: Monster

Threat Level: High

The hell hound lives and hunts in packs, but unlike its canine relative – the wolf - it doesn't bay or growl or snarl. Instead they are almost silent creatures, and that makes them very deadly indeed.

Stats: Fighting 7, Defence 14, Health 45, Damage 1-6 (1 dice)

Special Rules: The hell hound can breathe fire at a single target once every 3 combat rounds; they can do this even if they attack. The hell hound makes a Fighting roll and, if it hits, inflicts 1-6 (1 dice) damage upon the victim.

Hippogriff

The hippogriff is the result of magical animal experiments that took place in a time long forgot. This mysterious hybrid animal is the fusion of an eagle; head, front talons and wings and a riding horse; body, rear legs and tail.

Through its relatively short evolution the hippogriff is just as likely to be someone's steed, a griffon's dinner or a deadly predator. They are found in grassy regions where they herd together much like their normal equine relatives. If captured as an egg and reared correctly, a hippogriff will make a wonderful mount and a trusted friend. That said however, trying to steal eggs from a herd can prove to be a deadly pastime. Hippogriffs will either attack from the air using their powerful front talons or bite with their razor sharp beak.

Stats: Fighting 6, Defence 12, Health 40, Damage 3-8 (1 dice +2)

Special Rules: These creatures can fly. Their eggs can be sold at markets for 50 gold coins each.

Typical Native Climate: Wilderness

Encounter Numbers: 1-2 (6-36 in a herd)

Treasure: None but their eggs can be sold

Creature Type: Monster

Threat Level: High

Hobgoblin

Hobgoblins are bigger, meaner cousins of the common goblin that differ in quite a few ways. A typical Hobgoblin stands taller than a human at 2 metres tall. Their skin is dark green with warty growths and their teeth are oversized.

They are mean and aggressive but at the same time intelligent and organised. Where as a typical goblin band will simply wade into a fight, Hobgoblins use tactical missile fire, flanking manoeuvres and, on occasion, magic.

Stats: Fighting 3, Defence 10 (plus armour), Health 4, Damage by weapon

Special Rules: In their dungeon lairs, one in a hundred hobgoblins will be a shaman. They have access to 1-3 spells chosen by the games master. Shamans have an effective Magic score of 4.

Typical Native Climate: Dungeons

Encounter Numbers: 1-6 (50+ in dungeon lairs)

Treasure: None to common (rich in lair)

Creature Type: Humanoid

Threat Level: Normal

Horse

Horses are found all over the world, from the grasslands where they roam freely to cities and towns where they are used as mounts.

Stats: Fighting 3, Defence 10, Health 8, Damage 1-6 (1 dice)

Special Rules: None
Typical Native Climate: Any
Encounter Numbers: 1-20
Treasure: None
Creature Type: Animal
Threat Level: Normal

Hydra

A hydra is a large, snake-like creature with seven heads. Their long heads grow up to three metres in length and protrude from a huge lizard-like body. It is said that their blood contains a venom that burns those it touches; it is also said that when one of its heads is cut off, two more grow back to take its place. This has led many to believe that hydras are immortal.

A hydra can be found inhabiting swamps and other damp areas. They are solitary creatures and are highly aggressive, attacking any that dare venture near their lairs.

Stats: Fighting 5, Defence 16, Health 70, Damage 3-8 (1 dice + 2)

Special Rules: At the start of a hydra's turn, if they have suffered any damage in previous turns they heal 1-6 Health (roll 1 die). This does not apply if the hydra suffered any damage from fire since its last turn, however.

The blood of a hydra is toxic. Anyone causing damage to a hydra with a sharp weapon in hand-to-hand combat loses 1 Health.

Typical Native Climate: Swamp

Encounter Numbers: 1 (these are solitary monsters but can be found with young).

Treasure: Lair 1

Creature Type: Monster

Threat Level: Very High

Kobold

Kobolds are a race of miniature humanoids with tails. They stand barely 1 metre tall with brown scaly skin and long fingers and toes. Their heads are very dog-like as is their native language, which sounds like a small dog yapping. These creatures are very unclean and tend to smell ... well much like a wet dog.

Because of their small size and unkempt look the kobold is rarely taken seriously. This is a huge mistake! What these tiny monsters loose in size they make up in trickery and numbers. Kobolds are not at all stupid and wont attack unless they outnumber their opponent at least 3 to 1. Kobolds hate gnomes and will attack them on site.

Stats: Fighting 2, Defence 10, Health 2, Damage 1-3 (1 dice -3)

Special Rules: None

Typical Native Climate: Dungeons and wilderness

Encounter Numbers: 3 – 18 (400+ in their dungeon lairs)

Treasure: Sparse (Wealthy with the leader in their lair)

Creature Type: Humanoid

Threat Level: Low

Kraken

In the heart of every port you will find a tavern populated by old seadogs. Almost every one of these old seafarers will tell you a tale of ships being snatched out of the sea by a huge, multi-tentacle sea monster. This sea monster goes by the name of Kraken. The stories are grossly exaggerated of course. Description wise, a kraken is simply a giant squid. They grow to some 20 metres in length and although not quite big enough to pull ships under, they have been known to snatch sailors from the deck and devour them in a single bite!

Stats: Fighting 10, Defence 15, Health 100, Damage 3-18 (3 dice)

Special Rules: Before a Kraken can bite its prey with its huge beak, it must first attempt to grab a victim with one of its tentacles. The kraken must make a Fighting roll. If it is successful it has grabbed a victim. The victim must make a Strength roll with a Difficulty of 14 to break free. The victim can try to break free every round but it will take an automatic 3 damage from the bite.

Typical Native Climate: Ocean

Encounter Numbers: 1

Treasure: Lair 3 (but this will be some 2-3 kilometres beneath the sea!)

Creature Type: Monster

Threat Level: Extreme

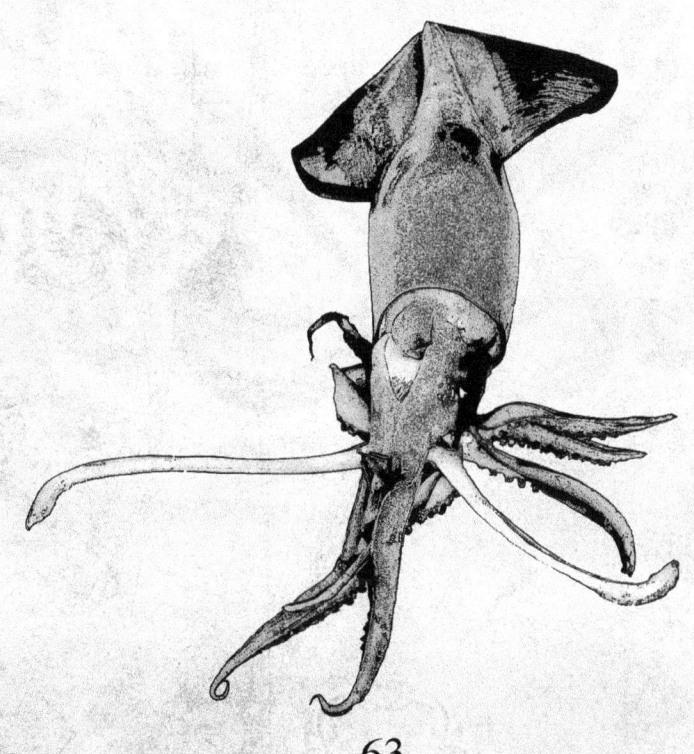

Leprechaun

This breed of fun-loving people is only half a metre tall. They can be found in green pastures, woods or forests. Male leprechauns have small wispy beards and dress in green clothes with a top hat and pointed shoes. They try to avoid combat at all costs and prefer to spend their time playing practical jokes on passersby. If threatened they can turn invisible at will.

Leprechauns are masters of illusion and can create effects that will make even the most powerful mage look twice. Even this fact, however, doesn't stop people searching them out, for it is rumoured that every leprechaun has a pot of gold or some other valuable treasure hidden away.

Stats: Fighting 2, Defence 10, Health 3, Damage by weapon -1

Special Rules: Leprechauns are masters of illusion. They have an effective Magic score of 10 and can cast the following spells at will:

Invisibility (Difficulty 12): This spell will make the leprechaun disappear into thin air. Only the keenest eye will spot the leprechaun as the spell bends light around him. The leprechaun can talk and act as normal wile under the effects of the spell. However, if he attempts to cast another spell or attack the spell will be broken. This spell lasts for 10 combat rounds. People actively looking for an invisible person must make a Magic roll (Difficulty 14). The leprechaun gains +3 to defence while invisible.

Create Illusion (Difficulty 13): The leprechaun can use this spell to create things that onlookers believe what they are seeing is actually real. The illusion can be absolutely anything at all: a huge dragon, a pot of gold, a castle in the clouds or simply a wall blocking some ones path. The illusion has full sound effects and even gives off an odour if need be. Of course, these things are not actually there and cannot cause any damage. Anyone viewing these illusions must make a Magic roll (Difficulty 14) to see through them. The spell can be broken by someone simply touching the illusion.

Typical Native Climate: Forests

Encounter Numbers: 3 – 18 (3 dice) or 100+ in woodland villages

Treasure: Lair 1

Creature Type: Humanoid

Threat Level: Low

Leviathan

There are many dangers lurking beneath the waves of the world's oceans. Some creatures, such as sea serpents and krakens are feared, and rightly so; they are large and dangerous and capable of sinking a ship. However, none are as feared as the almost mythical leviathan.

Many sailors dispute the fact that the leviathan even exists, as it is very rare that it is even seen. It sleeps for decades at a time, awakening only to satisfy its hunger. It looks somewhat like a massive, bloated serpent, with razor sharp teeth and eyes that are said to glow like twin full moons. But the most impressive thing about it is its size. The leviathan grows to over 100 metres long, making it the biggest creature in the world.

Stats: Fighting 12, Defence 16, Health 500, Damage 5-30 (5 dice)

Special Rules: None

Typical Native Climate: Oceans

Encounter Numbers: 1

Treasure: Lair 3, though it will be almost impossible to find

Creature Type: Monster

Threat Level: Off the charts!

Lich

Most men and women dream of having a long life. Some achieve this while others don't. However, some powerful and evil magicians use dark rituals to ensure that their life continues long passed the time it should have expired. These creatures are known as liches.

A lich often looks less like they did in life and more like some sort of undead creature – which is precisely what they have become. By using their necromancy they capture their life force in a vessel of some kind which they then hide in a safe place, for unless this vessel is destroyed, the lich cannot die. Even should their physical forms be 'killed', their life force will transfer to a new host and allow the lich to continue living their dark lives.

Stats: Fighting 9, Defence 11, Health 40, Damage 3-8 (1 dice +2)

Special Rules: A lich is a powerful magician and can cast all spells known to magicians, with an effective Magic score of 9. In addition, a lich is effectively immortal; if their bodies are destroyed their life force will transfer to another body. The target can resist with a Charisma roll (Difficulty 10), though they will be unaware of what is actually happening. Only by destroying the vessel can the lich be truly killed.

Typical Native Climate: Any

Encounter Numbers: 1

Treasure: Lair 2

Creature Type: Undead

Threat Level: Very high

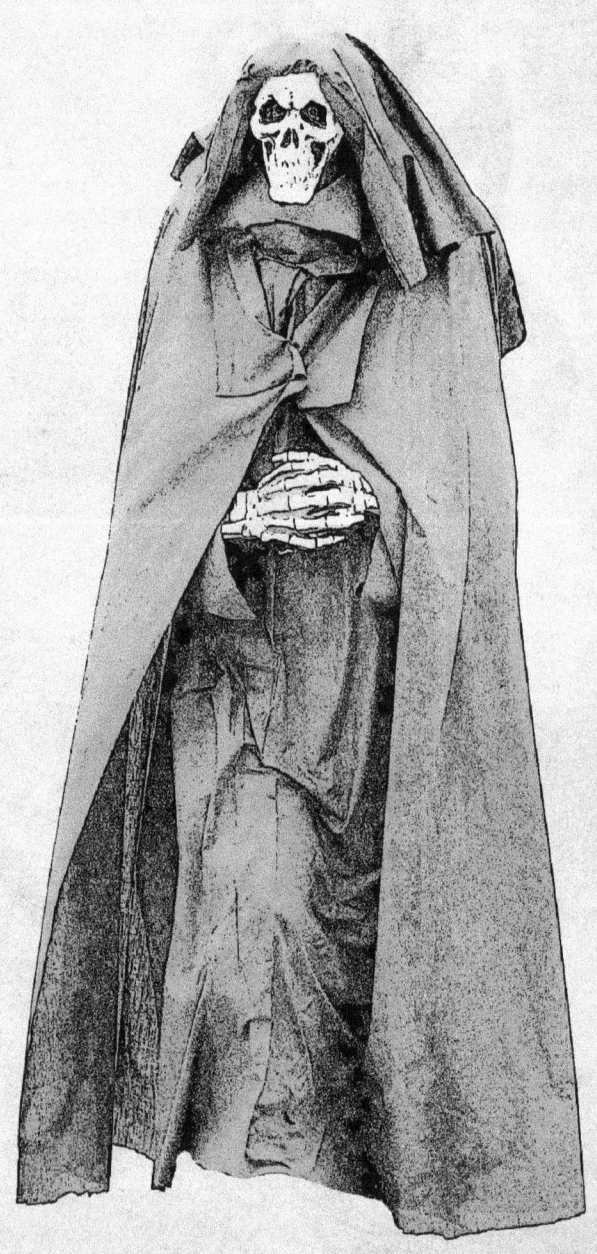

Lion

Probably the strongest of the great cats, the lion is a majestic beast that hunts the plains and savannahs of the world, stalking its prey.

Stats: Fighting 5, Defence 11, Health 15, Damage 3-8 (1 dice +2)

Special Rules: None

Typical Native Climate: Plains

Encounter Numbers: 1

Treasure: None

Creature Type: Animal

Threat Level: High

Mammoth

Mammoths are elephant-like creatures, though much larger. They are covered in thick white hair which protects them from the extreme cold of the tundras and snow plains where they live. They are very dangerous enemies as their thick tusks can impale a man and their large feet can trample him.

Hunters and poachers often mount expeditions into the colder climes of the world in search of mammoths. The ivory of their tusks brings large prices in the more exotic markets of the world.

Stats: Fighting 6, Defence 16, Health 60, Damage 2-12 (2 dice)

Special Rules: Every time the mammoth attacks, roll a dice. On a 5 or 6 it decides to trample. It may make one attack against all man-sized opponents it is in hand-to-hand combat with.

Typical Native Climate: Tundra

Encounter Numbers: 1-3 (1 dice divided by 2)

Treasure: None

Creature Type: Animal

Threat Level: Very high

Manticore

Many people consider the manticore to be a myth, a creature made-up to scare small children. This is not true, as the manticore is very real indeed. It has the body of a large lion, the tail of a scorpion and, most disturbingly of all, the head and face of a bearded man. Two bat-like wings protrude from its shoulders, allowing it to fly. Its voice is sweet, an attribute it uses to lure the unwary to it where it then kills and devours them (this has lead to the manticore often being referred to as the 'man-eater').

Stats: Fighting 9, Defence 14, Health 50, Damage 2-12 (2 dice)

Special Rules: Manticores are able to shoot their tail spikes at opponents. This is used as a ranged combat attack and inflicts 1-6 damage (roll 1 dice).

Typical Native Climate: Desert or jungle

Encounter Numbers: 1

Treasure: None

Creature Type: Monster

Threat Level: Very High

Merman

A merman (and a mermaid) is a half-human, half-fish creature that lives in the seas and oceans of the world. From the waist up they have the body, arms and head of a man or woman, with coral green eyes and green, seaweed-like hair. From the waist down they are all fish, having no legs but instead a fish tail.

Mermen and mermaids can often be seen frolicking in the waves or playing with dolphins. They are usually harmless unless threatened. However, they will occasionally go out of their way to lure a human into the water. When this happens the victim becomes a new merman or mermaid; this is the only way these creatures can reproduce.

It is rumoured that an underwater city exists somewhere beneath the waves that is home to these creatures. This has never been proven conclusively however.

Stats: Fighting 3, Defence 10, Health 4, Damage by weapon

Special Rules: Mermen and mermaids have the innate ability to allow other creatures to breath underwater if they so choose. They are also able to cast the following spell, with an effective Magic score of 7.

Allure (Difficulty 12): This spell allows the merman or mermaid to charm other people into approaching her. The victim is allowed to make a Charisma roll (Difficulty 12) to resist the effects, or else he must approach the caster. This will usually lead to the victim becoming a merman or mermaid.

Typical Native Climate: Oceans

Encounter Numbers: 1-6 (1 dice) or 20+

Treasure: Sparse to Wealthy

Creature Type: Humanoid

Threat Level: Normal

Minotaur

A minotaur is a creature that is part man and part bull. They have the body, arms and legs of a well-muscled human, while the head is that of a raging bull. They are violent and aggressive, a fact that many that have crossed their paths have found out, usually the hard way.

Minotaurs are usually found underground or in caves. Some powerful men and women have managed to attract the services of a minotaur with promises of power and food.

Stats: Fighting 5, Defence 11, Health 15, Damage 2-7 (1 dice + 1)

Special Rules: As soon as a minotaur loses Health they fly into a frenzy of bloodlust. They gain a +1 bonus to their Fighting score, but their Defence is reduced by -1 for the remainder of the combat.

Typical Native Climate: Dungeons

Encounter Numbers: 1-6 (1 dice)

Treasure: Common

Creature Type: Humanoid

Threat Level: Normal

Nymph

The nymph is a female water spirit that lives in streams, lakes and springs of pure, untainted water. They appear as a beautiful young woman, with long, flowing golden hair that cascades down their backs. They wear white, semi-transparent clothing designed to reveal their bodies.

Many are the dangers of encountering a nymph, especially for males. Nymphs have an insatiable urge to mate, but they cannot leave the water. Therefore, a nymph will often lure an unsuspecting person into the water to mate with her, where the victim will thus drown.

If a nymph encounters a beautiful female, the nymph will often be overcome with jealousy and use the same trick to lure that victim into the water, where the nymph will attempt to kill her.

Stats: Fighting 1, Defence 10. Health 5, Damage 1-3 (1 dice divided by 2)

Special Rules: Nymphs may cast the following spell, with an effective Magic score of 9.

Allure (Difficulty 12): This spell allows the nymph to charm other people into approaching her. The victim is allowed to make a Charisma roll (Difficulty 12) to resist the effects, or else he must approach the nymph. This will usually lead to the victim's death at the hands of the nymph through drowning.

Typical Native Climate: Fresh water streams, lakes and ponds.

Encounter Numbers: 1-6 (1 dice)

Treasure: Rich

Creature Type: Humanoid

Threat Level: Normal

Ogre

Ogres are a vicious race of humanoids with a fondness for eating human flesh. They are brutish, mean and vicious, often cooking their victims alive.

A typical ogre is about 2 and a half metres tall. They are strong and often have fat bellies from all the food they eat. They live in forests, hills and caves; every evening they go hunting for food. They will eat just about anything, but will take human flesh over anything else.

Stats: Fighting 4, Defence 12 (plus armour), Health 13, Damage by weapon +1

Special Rules: None

Typical Native Climate: Forests and mountains

Encounter Numbers: 1 or 1-6 in lair (1 dice)

Treasure: Sparse

Creature Type: Humanoid

Threat Level: Normal

Orc

Orcs are larger, more brutish relations of goblins. Standing about two metres tall, they are ugly, misshapen brutes. Their skin colour ranges from brown to dark green to black. Although not very intelligent, they are strong and tough, which suits their aggressive, warlike disposition perfectly. Orc tribes are usually found living in hilly or wooded areas, though they are frequently encountered in the lands of other civilizations as they raid and pillage.

Some scholars say that orcs are descended from elves who experimented in dark magic and became twisted and corrupt in the process; this is not know for certain, though there is certainly a hatred that exists between the two races.

Stats: Fighting 3, Defence 11 (plus armour), Health 4, Damage by weapon

Special Rules: None

Typical Native Climate: Forests, mountains and dungeons

Encounter Numbers: 1-6 (1 dice) or 50+ in tribal settlements

Treasure: Common or lair 1

Creature Type: Humanoid

Threat Level: Normal

Panther

The panther is a sleek and fierce hunter, often hiding in the shadows of the jungle before launching itself towards its prey with unerring precision.

Stats: Fighting 5, Defence 10, Health 10, Damage 2-7 (1 dice +1)

Special Rules: A panther may add +2 to its dice roll to determine initiative.

Typical Native Climate: Jungle

Encounter Numbers: 1

Treasure: None

Creature Type: Animal

Threat Level: Normal

Pegasus

On the surface, a pegasus looks like nothing more than a winged horse. However, there is much more to them than this. It is said that the first pegasus was born when the sun goddess fell in love with a mighty stallion and gave it wings so that it might fly up to see her. The stallion did this and in its new home amongst the gods became wise and noble. The descendants of that stallion inherited the same traits, giving rise to a majestic race of winged horses.

These days a pegasus can be found living high in the mountains or roaming the open plains. They are good creatures and have no time for evil whatsoever.

Stats: Fighting 4, Defence 11, Health 24, Damage 2-7 (1 dice +1)

Special Rules: None

Typical Native Climate: Mountains or plains

Encounter Numbers: 1-3 (1 dice divided by 2)

Treasure: None

Creature Type: Monster

Threat Level: Normal

Phoenix

Also known as the firebird, a phoenix is a rare and fantastic creature encountered only very rarely. They are large creatures, with a wingspan greater of that than a giant eagle. Their feathers are a rich scarlet colour, with flecks of purple and blue, and their tale is a magnificent gold. They are found only in the highest mountains.

A phoenix has a very long life of around one thousand years. When a phoenix dies, their bodies burst into a flame of intense heat. Before long, all that remains of the magnificent bird is a pile of ashes. This is not the end for the phoenix however, for a short time later a new, young phoenix will emerge from the ashes.

The phoenix is a peaceful creature, though it will fight to protect itself if it needs to. Capturing a phoenix, especially a young one, has become a quest for many young adventurers, though to actually accomplish it would be a great feat indeed.

Stats: Fighting 9, Defence 13, Health 45, Damage 2-12 (2 dice)

Special Rules: A phoenix is extremely hard to kill, leading many to believe it is immortal. At the start of each turn of combat, a phoenix will automatically heal 2-12 (2 dice) Health.

If a phoenix is killed, its body bursts into flames, scorching any who were in combat with it. Those who are lose 2-12 Health (2 dice). The phoenix will collapse into a pile of ashes but will be reborn 48 hours later.

Typical Native Climate: Mountains

Encounter Numbers: 1

Treasure: None

Creature Type: Monster

Threat Level: Very High

Pixie

The pixie is a small fairy creature found only in enchanted glens in the middle of ancient forests. Sometimes they will be found living with or near elves, but this is much rarer.

A pixie is humanoid in appearance though extremely small; usually only twenty to thirty centimetres in height. In all respects they look like a miniature elf, except that they have fine, gossamer wings that allow them to flitter through the air like a butterfly. They always appear nude, preferring to be one with nature rather than wear clothing.

Pixies do not usually prove a danger to anyone. If anything, they are more of an annoyance than a danger, as a pixie has a wicked sense of humour and likes to play practice jokes. They have a fondness for children, and some pixies have accidently caused young boys and girls to become lost in the woods after luring them in there to play.

Stats: Fighting 1, Defence 10, Health 1, Damage 1

Special Rules: Pixies are tricksters and illusionists. They have an effective Magic score of 10 and can cast the following spells at will:

Invisibility (Difficulty 12): This spell will make the pixie disappear into thin air. Only the keenest eye will spot the pixie as the spell bends light around him. The pixie can talk and act as normal wile under the effects of the spell. However, if he attempts to cast another spell or attack the spell will be broken. This spell lasts for 10 combat rounds. People actively looking for an invisible person must make a Magic roll (Difficulty 14). The pixie gains +3 to defence while invisible.

Create Illusion (Difficulty 13): The pixie can use this spell to create things that onlookers believe what they are seeing is actually real. The illusion can be absolutely anything at all: a huge dragon, a pot of gold, a castle in the clouds or simply a wall blocking some ones path. The illusion has full sound effects and even gives off an odour if need be. Of course, these things are not actually there and cannot cause any damage. Anyone viewing these illusions must make a Magic roll (Difficulty 14) to see through them. The spell can be broken by someone simply touching the illusion.

Typical Native Climate: Forests

Encouter Numbers: 3-18 (3 dice)

Treasure: None

Creature Type: Humanoid

Threat Level: Low

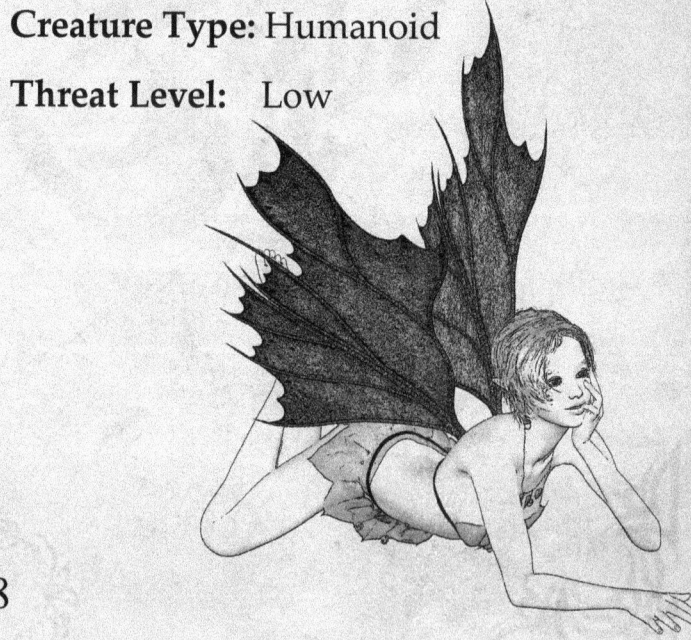

Rakshasa

Said to be a form of demon, them rakshasa (or rakshasi for the female version) is a supernatural, evil humanoid creature. They are able to change their appearance at will, and no one is quite sure what the natural appearance of a rakshasa actually is, though many scholars speculate that they look like a demonic tiger-man, with black fur and curved horns protruding from their heads. This is speculation though, and most rakshasas will appear as a human or elf when encountered.

Unlike normal demons, which are aggressive and impulsive, rakshasas are organized and disciplined. They are powerful warriors fight like professional soldiers, in an ordered and well-drilled manners. They are also powerful spellcasters, and can resort to magic when their steel fails them.

Stats: Fighting 5, Defence 12, Health 18, Damage by weapon +1

Special Rules: Rakshasas are capabale spell casters. They have an effective magic score of 6 and can cast the same spells as a magician. In addition they may cast the following spell.

Transformation (Difficulty 13): This spell allows the rakshasa to transform into another humanoid. The assumed form can be either completely random (between the heights of 0.5 and 2 metres) or it can be a copy of someone the rakshasa has recently seen. If the rakshasa copies someone and then attempts to assume their life or pretend to be them for a while, there is a chance that someone close to the copied victim (a relative or close friend) may smell a rat. If the rakshasa, in his copied form, does something 'out of character' for the copied person, the relative or friend can make a Knowledge roll (Difficulty 12). If successful, they will realise a fatal flaw in the rakshasa's transformation.

Typical Native Climate: Any

Encounter Numbers: 1-6 (1 dice)

Treasure: Common

Creature Type: Humanoid

Threat Level: High

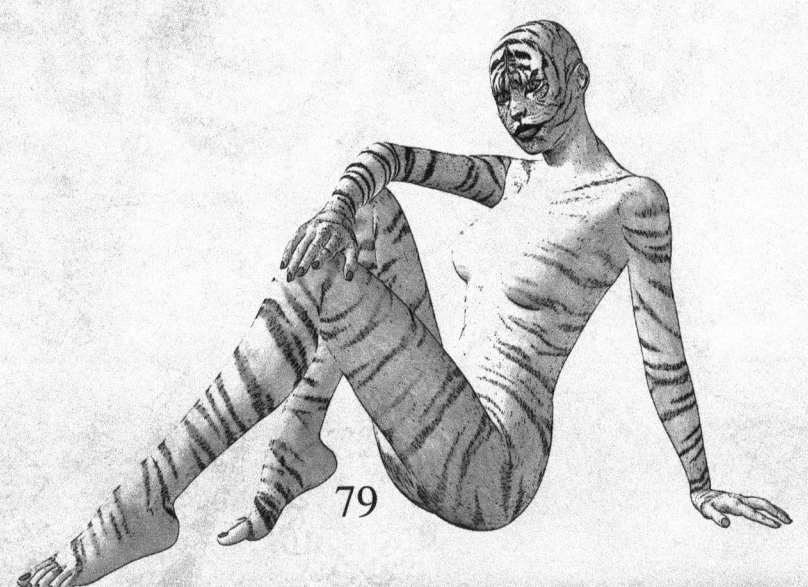

Satyr

In the depths of the largest forests you can find many strange creatures, one of which is the satyr. Here the frolic, often with nymphs to whom the species has close relations. They are fond of good wine and drink it in copious amounts, which often means that they are drunk when encountered. They also love music and are adept at playing the pipes; in fact, the first sign of a satyr in the area is often the sound of pipe music echoing through the trees. Most satyrs are shy and reclusive and don't usually pose a danger to travellers unless threatened.

A satyr looks like a human male except from the waist down where they instead have the legs of a goat. Their heads are crowned with two small horns, and a long, wispy beard grows from their faces.

Stats: Fighting 3, Defence 10, Health 6, Damage 1-6 (1 dice)

Special Rules: None

Typical Native Climate: Forests

Encounter Numbers: 1-6 (1 dice)

Treasure: Sparse

Creature Type: Humanoid

Threat Level: Normal

Sea Serpent

Within the briny depths of the seas and oceans live many dangerous creatures. Most never trouble ships, but some, like the massive water snakes known as sea serpents, have a nasty habit of doing just that.

Sea serpents are massive, growing anywhere up to five metres long. They rise up out of the water to attack passing ships, hungry to devour the crew for they crave the taste of warm flesh. They often raise their massive heads up high and bring them down across the deck of the ship in an attempt to smash it to pieces, and then eat the crew at its leisure.

Stats: Fighting 6, Defence 12, Health 27, Damage 3-8 (1 dice +2)

Special Rules: None

Typical Native Climate: Oceans

Encounter Numbers: 1-3 (1 dice divided by 2)

Treasure: None or Lair 2

Creature Type: Monster

Threat Level: High

Skeleton

Skeletons are the reanimated bones of the dead. Held together by evil magic, these creatures are under the complete control of their creator. They are mindless and relentless and will fight no matter the odds.

Although most skeletons resemble humans (these are the easiest forms to reanimate), other types of skeletons, such as orcs, elves, gnomes, even giants are possible. Animal skeletons are also commonly used.

Stats: Fighting 2, Defence 10, Health 5, Damage by weapon

Special Rules: These creatures are hard to hurt with bladed weapons. Unless the weapon their enemy is using is blunt, reduce all damage done to them by 1.

Typical Native Climate: Any

Encounter Numbers: 2-12 (2 dice)

Treasure: None

Creature Type: Undead

Threat Level: Low

Slaver

In many parts of the world the act of buying and selling slaves is an illegal trade. But that doesn't stop people from doing this heinous crime. Slavers are men and women who trade in slaves, buying and selling them at clandestine markets organized in the larger cities of the world. How they come to acquire their slaves is also a grey area, for many of them hire thugs and kidnappers to abduct and subdue potential slaves before locking them in chains and dragging them off to the markets.

Stats: Fighting 2, Defence 10 (plus armour), Health 4, Damage by weapon

Special Rules: None

Typical Native Climate: Urban, but could be anywhere

Encounter Numbers: 1, plus 2-12 thugs (2 dice)

Treasure: Rich

Creature Type: Humanoid

Threat Level: Normal

Soldier

Every society, every race, has some sort of army. The bulk of these armies are made up of professional warriors, men and women payed to serve their king and country. These people are called soldiers.

People join the army for all sorts of reasons, but upon joining they begin training in earnest for their now job. They learn not only how to use a variety of weapons, shields and how to wear armour, but also how to fight as a group rather than an individual. This training pays off on the field of battle, as they can support their fellow soldiers and be supported themselves.

Stats: Fighting 3, Defence 10 (plus armour), Health 5, Damage by weapon

Special Rules: If two or more soldiers are facing the same opponent in hand-to-hand combat, all of those soldiers gain +1 Fighting due to their training.

Typical Native Climate: Any

Encounter Numbers: Anywhere from 1-100

Treasure: Common

Creature Type: Humanoid

Threat Level: Normal

Sphinx

A sphinx is a large creature that looks much like a massive lioness, except that it has the head of a female human. They are said to be agents of the gods, sent down to the mortal world to guard and watch over areas the gods hold sacred or do not want disturbed. They will sit at their designated place until the gods say otherwise, not allowing anyone to pass unless they can first prove themselves worthy. This can be done by answering a riddle that the sphinx devises. If it can be answered, that person will be allowed to continue into the area the sphinx is guarding. If it cannot be answered, the sphinx will not allow the person to pass, attacking if they try to force their way through.

Stats: Fighting 8, Defence 16, Health 50, Damage 2-12 (2 dice)

Special Rules: None

Typical Native Climate: Any

Encounter Numbers: 1-2

Treasure: Rich

Creature Type: Monster

Threat Level: Very High

Tiger

Fearsome and mighty, those travelling through the jungles of the world need to beware of the tiger. These great cats hunt their prey alone, pouncing upon them before rending them with their teeth and claws.

Stats: Fighting 5, Defence 11, Health 12, Damage 2-7 (1 dice +1)

Special Rules: None

Typical Native Climate: Jungle

Encounter Numbers: 1

Treasure: None

Creature Type: Animal

Threat Level: Normal

Titan

The titans are a race of greater giants. Once populous in number, the titan race has now dwindled to a very small number; some scholars think as few as twenty titans now survive. This is not due to old age, as titans live more than one thousand years. Mainly it is due to their war with their lesser kin, the giants.

Many years ago the giants declared war on their cousins. What provoked this is unknown, but the giants, with their superior numbers, won the war after many, many years. Now the titan race is dwindling and on the verge of extinction.

Titans look just like giants, except they grow up to 10 metres tall. They are not an overly aggressive race, but will attack with fury if anything happens to threaten their already tenuous existence.

Stats: Fighting 8, Defence 18, Health 130, Damage 3-18 (3 dice)

Special Rules: None

Typical Native Climate: Mountains

Encounter Numbers: 1

Treasure: Wealthy

Creature Type: Humanoid

Threat Level: Extreme

TREEMAN

Some travellers, when walking through an ancient forest, feel as though they are being watched. Some put this down to elves, some to animals and some to simple paranoia. Not many actually realize that it is the trees themselves doing the watching.

Calling themselves the watchers of the woods, treemen are a race of sentient trees that are actually intelligent, living beings. They are as old as the forests themselves. The look like ordinary trees, with barky skin and branches with leaves. However, they have a set of eyes halfway up their 'trunks', and a mouth just below it. When they speak it is in a deep, low and slow voice that sounds like the creaking of timber. When they move it is with slow, ponderous strides that shakes the ground.

Treemen are normally content to watch and observe intruders in the forests they protect. However, should one of these intruders do something that could harm the woods or its inhabitants in any way they will be roused into anger and act with haste.

Stats: Fighting 8, Defence 17, Health 70, Damage 2-12 (2 dice)

Special Rules: Treemen are highly flammable creatures. Should they suffer any damage from a fire source, that damage is doubled.

Typical Native Climate: Forests

Encounter Numbers: 1-3 (1 dice divided by 2)

Treasure: None

Creature Type: Monster

Threat Level: Extreme

Troll

Trolls are hideously ugly, stunted, giant-like creatures. They have warty skin, bulbous nose and long, unkempt hair. Their ears are large, as are their bellies; almost all trolls are rather fat. They stand about 3 metres tall and are heavily muscled. They are not very smart, however, but they are very aggressive and are likely to attack a passerby on sight.

Normally found in marshes and swamps, trolls sometimes venture out of their lairs in search of food. However they only move about at night, as they hate the bright warmth of the sun.

Stats: Fighting 5, Defence 11, Health 30, Damage 3-8 (1 dice + 2)

Special Rules: Trolls who end up having to fight in daylight suffer a -1 penalty to both their Fighting and Defence scores for the duration of the fight.

Trolls also have a natural healing ability that means that wounds close up faster than those of other creatures. Therefore, any damage dealt to a troll is reduced by 1.

Typical Native Climate: Swamps

Encounter Numbers: 1-6 (1 dice)

Treasure: Sparse to Wealthy

Creature Type: Humanoid

Threat Level: High

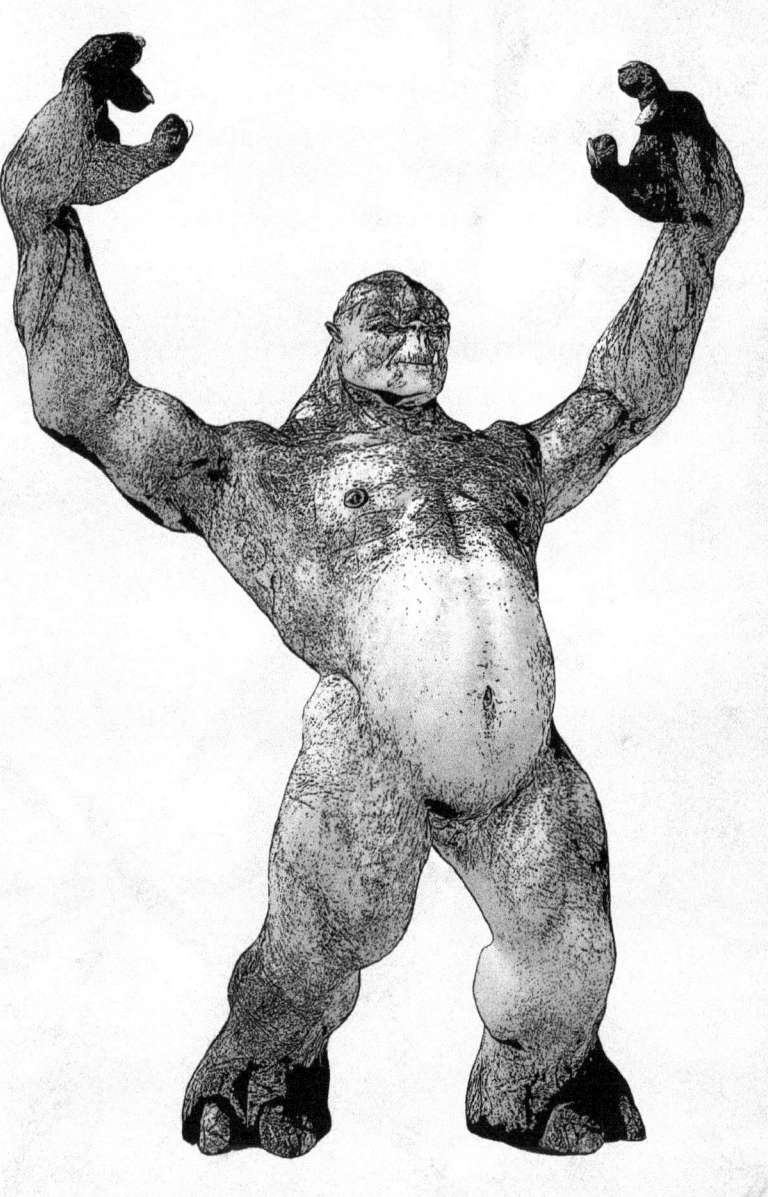

Unicorn

A unicorn looks like a very large horse, standing over 2 and a half metres tall. Where it differs from a horse in appearance is that it has cloven hooves, a tail similar to that of a lion, and a long white beard. It also has a single horn protruding from its forehead.

It is said that this horn provides the unicorn with many powers and for this reason unicorn hunting is a popular pastime. However not many are ever caught as these creatures are wise and intelligent and often outsmart would-be hunters. They live in deep forests where they prefer to keep to themselves, but they have been known to help out those with pure intentions on occasion.

Stats: Fighting 6, Defence 11, Health 30, Damage 2-12 (2 dice)

Special Rules: The horn of a unicorn provides it with certain abilities. Firstly, any magical spell cast against it has its Difficulty score increased by 2, making it much harder for the unicorn to be affected. Secondly, it makes the unicorn immune to poisons. Finally it allows the unicorn to detect any creatures with evil intentions near it.

Typical Native Climate: Forest

Encounter Numbers: 1

Treasure: Lair 1

Creature Type: Monster

Threat Level: High

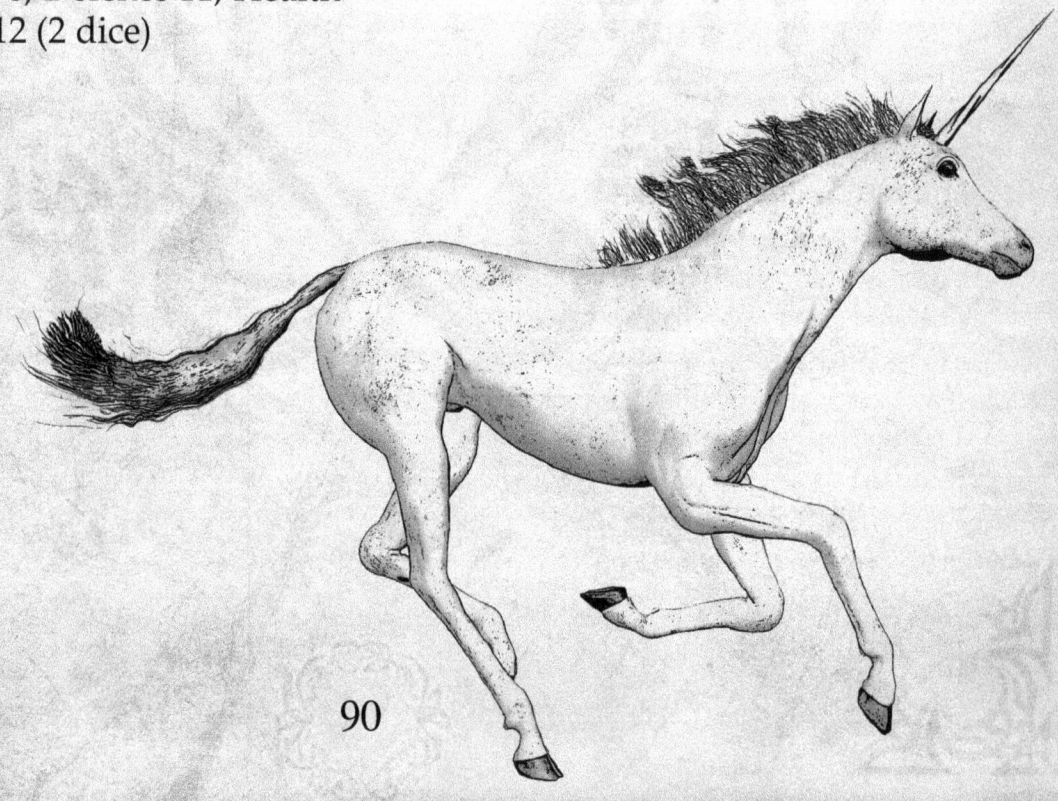

Vampire

Vampires are undead creatures that drink the blood of their victims. This ritual keeps them 'alive' and youthful.

Many vampires cannot be distinguished from normal creatures of their race. Some signs that a creature may be a vampire include an aversion to sunlight, pale skin or behaving oddly at the sight of blood, a substance they crave. Other than those things vampires often live normal lives amongst society, sometimes even as nobles or lords.

Vampires are immortal creatures, unable to be permanently killed by normal means. The only way to destroy a vampire forever is to expose them to sunlight, cut of their head with a weapon made of silver, or drive a wooden stake through their heart. If a vampire is killed in any other way, they will simply resurrect the following night at midnight.

Stats: Fighting 9. Defence 16, Health 40, Damage 2-12 (2 dice)

Special Rules: A vampire reduced to 0 Health will come back to life at midnight the following night. Only if they are killed by the methods mentioned above will this not occur.

During their turn, a vampire can choose to drink the blood of a victim he has wounded during combat instead of attacking. The vampire instantly heals 2-12 Health (roll 2 dice).

A vampire exposed to direct sunlight, or in the presence of a holy symbol, loses 1-6 Health each turn of exposure (roll 1 dice). The same applies if there is a clove of garlic within smelling distance.

Typical Native Climate: Any

Encounter Numbers: 1

Treasure: Wealthy to Lair 3

Creature Type: Undead

Threat Level: Very High

WARHOUND

Warhounds are trained attack dogs. Often used by armies, a warhound is trained from birth to obey its handler. In combat they attack on command, only stopping when their handler tells them too.

Stats: Fighting 4, Defence 10, Health 6, Damage 1-6 (1 dice)

Special Rules: None

Typical Native Climate: Any

Encounter Numbers: 2-12 (2 dice)

Creature Type: Animal

Threat Level: Normal

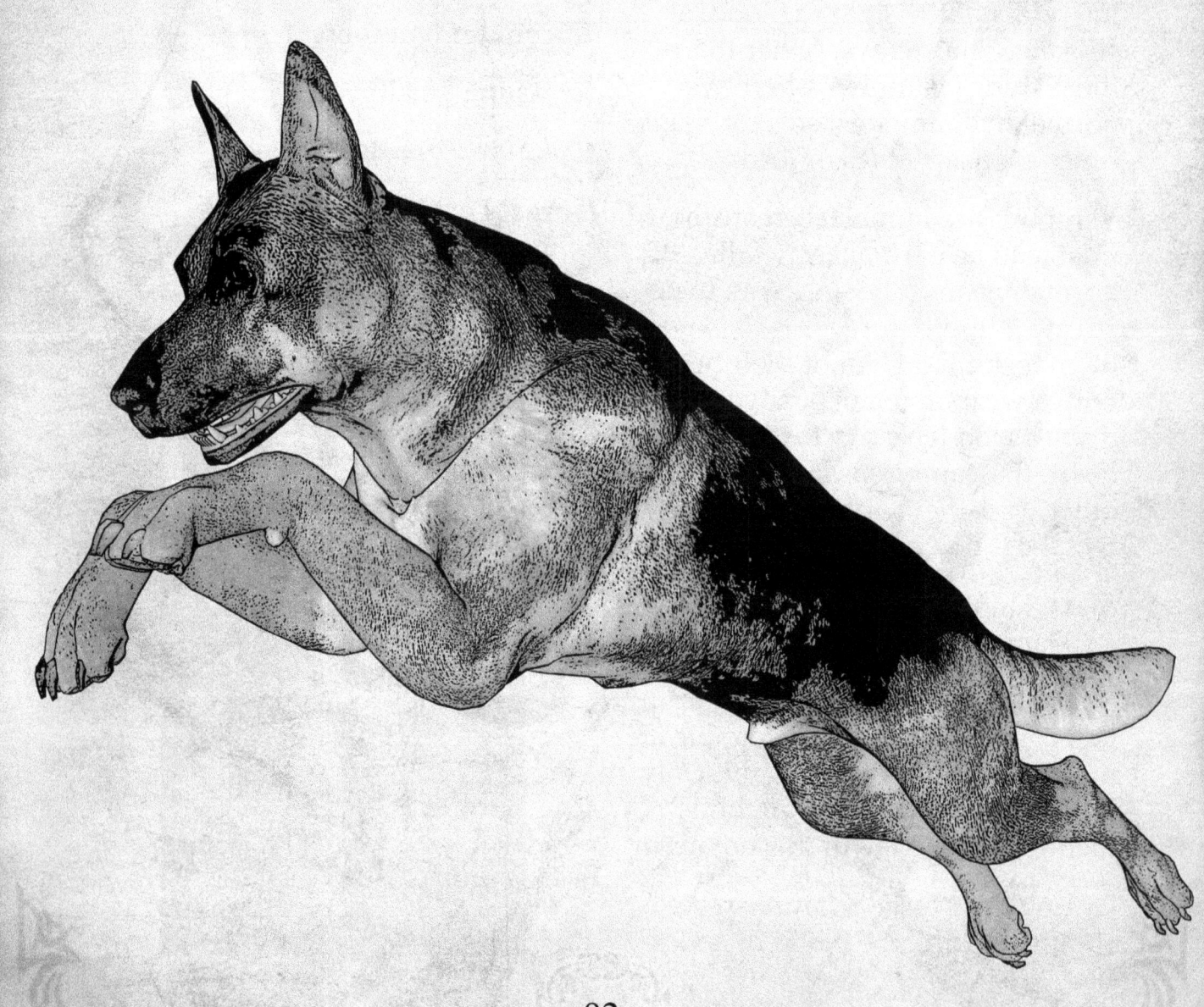

Werewolf

Every man, woman and child knows that when the full moon rises, it is time to head inside and to lock the doors. For on those nights, the werewolves prowl.

A werewolf is a man or woman who has been infected with a disease known as lycanthropy. This is usually contracted by being bitten by a werewolf. Once this has occurred, every full moon as the sun goes down they will transform into a wolf-man and go on a feeding frenzy. They have no control over this; it happens whether they like it or not.

There is no known cure for lycanthropy, though it is said that a sprig of belladonna, administered to a werewolf bite immediately, will stop the victim from becoming infected.

Stats: Fighting 4, Defence 10, Health 10, Damage 1-6 (1 dice)

Special Rules: Anyone damaged by a werewolf in hand-to-hand combat will become a werewolf themselves on the next full moon, unless they use a sprig of belladonna to prevent this before that occurs.

Typical Native Climate: Urban or forests

Encounter Numbers: 1-6 (1 dice)

Creature Type: Monster

Treasure: Sparse

Threat Level: Normal

Will-o'-the-Wisp

Travellers through the bogs and marshes of the world often tell tales of strange lights that they see. These lights, sometimes called ghost lights or fay lights, are said to dance and sway through the air, enticing those who see them to follow. The wise avoid them at all costs; the foolish or ignorant follow after them out of curiosity. Ultimately this leads to their downfall, for they inevitably become lost in the swamp.

It is impossible to fight a will-o'-the-wisp for they always move away from anyone approaching them. No one has ever been able to catch one.

Stats: No stats are given for a will-o'-the-wisp as they are impossible to fight.

Special Rules: None

Typical Native Climate: Swamp

Encounter Numbers: 1-6 (1 dice)

Treasure: None

Creature Type: Monster

Threat Level: Low

Wolf

Wolves prowl the mountains and forests of the world, hunting weaker animals for prey. They roam in packs, ganging up on their intended victims. Although they usually leave more powerful creatures alone they will sometimes attack them, especially if they are hungry and cannot find another source of food.

Stats: Fighting 3, Defence 10, Health 3, Damage 2-7 (1 dice +1)

Special Rules: If two or more wolves are facing the same opponent in hand-to-hand combat, all of those wolves gain +1 Fighting.

Typical Native Climate: Forests and mountains

Encounter Numbers: 2-12 (2 dice)

Treasure: None

Creature Type: Animal

Threat Level: Normal

Wraith

Wraiths are the undead spirits of very evil men or women who have died and been sent back to the world of the living by the dark gods. Usually this is done for a specific purpose, such as finishing an uncompleted task or gaining revenge on those who killed them. If this task is completed the wraith either returns to the afterlife or is free to wreck havoc upon the world as they see fit.

Stats: Fighting 4, Defence 11, Health 20, Damage 1-6 (1 dice)

Special Rules: Wraiths are ethereal creatures and are able to move through objects. Because of this, unless a creature fighting them is using a magical weapon, a wraith gains a +5 bonus to their Defence score.

The touch of a wraith drains the life force from its victim. Anyone damaged by a wraith not only takes normal damage but also loses 1 point from their maximum Health score (this is permanent).

Typical Native Climate: Any

Encounter Numbers: 1-6 (1 dice)

Treasure: None

Creature Type: Undead

Threat Level: High

Wyvern

At first glance a wyvern appears to be a small dragon. Both are serpentine in appearance, with long bodies, large wings and fang-filled jaws. But there the resemblance ends. Unlike dragons, wyverns do not possess front legs and feet, instead having only the two rear ones. They also lack the magical abilities, breath weapons and intelligence of their larger cousins. However, they do have a venomous sting on the tips of their tales which use to paralyse their prey.

Wyverns are often seen flying across mountains and hills, where they lair and make their nests. Wyvern eggs are highly sought after amongst collectors and they often pay handsomely for them.

Stats: Fighting 7, Defence 16, Health 45, Damage 3-8 (1 dice +2)

Special Rules: If a wyvern hits an opponent on hand-to-hand combat, roll a dice. On a 5-6 the victim has been struck with the wyvern's sting and must make a Strength roll (Difficulty 12) or be paralysed for five minutes of game time.

Typical Native Climate: Mountains

Encounter Numbers: 1-3 (1 dice divided by 2)

Treasure: Common

Creature Type: Monster

Threat Level: Very high

Yeti

The yeti is a rare, ape-like creature found only in cold, inhospitable climes. Known by many names (including man-bear, wild man or snow man) they are only seen occasionally by travellers. Some report that their camps are attacked in the night by the creatures, though no evidence has ever been found to confirm whether it is a yeti or some other creature that has done this.

The yeti is at least semi-intelligent, though they possess considerably less knowledge than humans. Some theorize that a yeti is half way between apes and humans on the evolutionary scale; this is just a theory however, though it does seem plausible.

Stats: Fighting 5, Defence 11, Health 20, Damage 2-7 (1 dice +1)

Special Rules: If a yeti rolls a double 6 on their Fighting roll then they have managed to hit with both of their massive fists. The yeti deals double damage for that turn.

Typical Native Climate: Mountains and tundra

Encounter Numbers: 1-6 (1 dice)

Treasure: Sparse

Creature Type: Monster

Threat Level: High

Zombie

Zombies are undead creatures created through the use of foul magic. They are the reanimated rotting corpses of the deceased, dug up by evil necromancers for use in their private armies. Shambling forward, zombies know no fear and will fight whatever their controller wants them to. In this way they are very reliable, as their creator knows they will never flee the field of battle.

Stats: Fighting 2, Defence 10, Health 5, Damage by weapon

Special Rules: None

Typical Native Climate: Any

Encounter Numbers: 2-12 (2 dice)

Treasure: None

Creature Type: Undead

Threat Level: Low

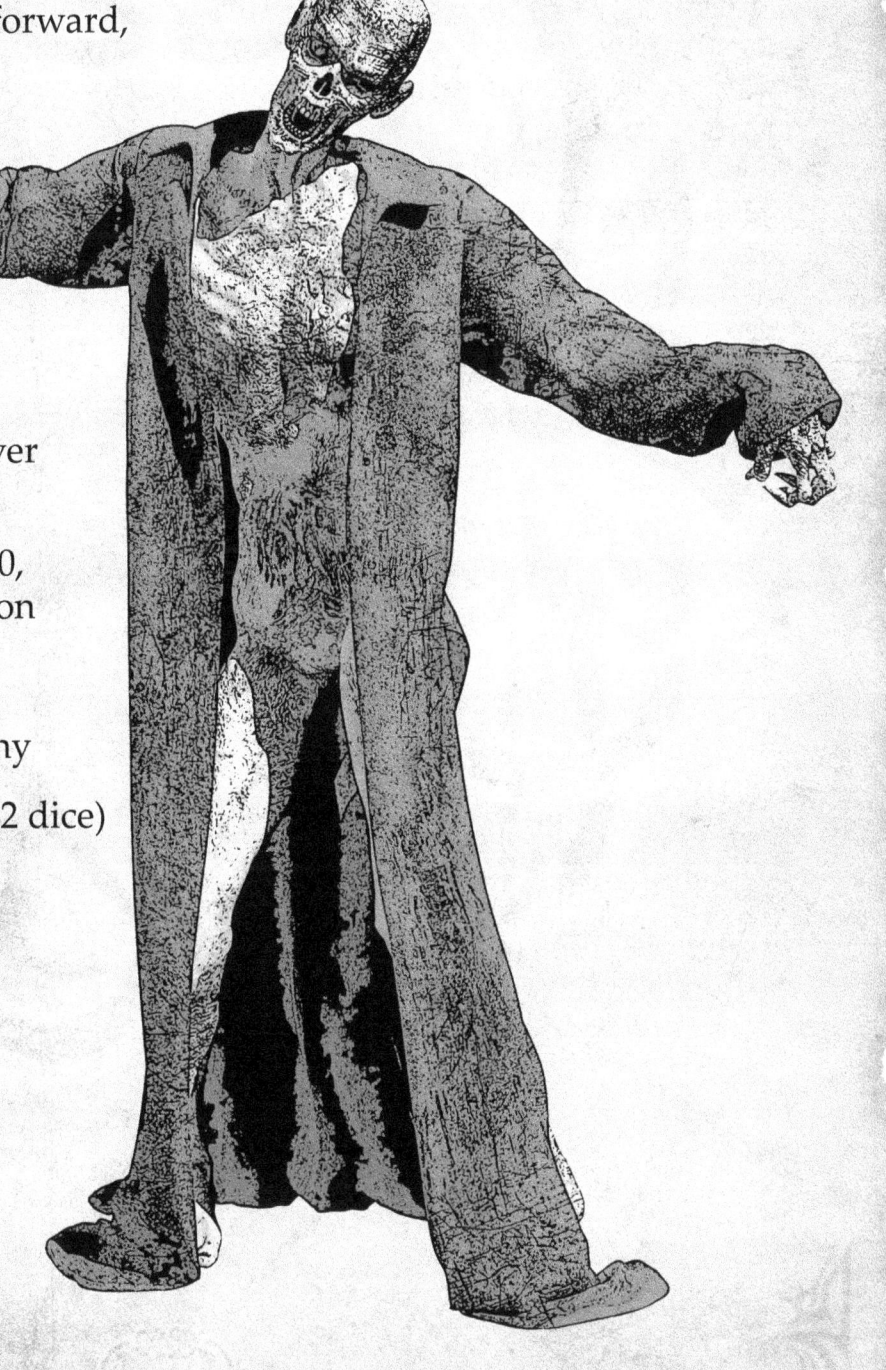

Appendix I

This section gives you two lists that Gamesmasters should find very useful. The first lists all of the monsters by their threat level. This allows you to pick monsters of the appropriate danger when creating your own adventures. Basically, if you follow the guidelines set out here, the monsters they encounter should be tough but fair.

A low threat level should not pose problems for a group of characters. They should be able to take on a group of these monsters comfortably.

A normal threat level should threaten a group of characters, but not overly so. They should still be able to beat a small group of them easily enough, though several groups of these one after the other could slowly whittle them down.

A single high threat level monster should be able to be tackled by a group of characters without too many dramas. A group of high threat level monsters will pose problems unless the characters are experienced.

Only groups of experienced characters should tackle a very high threat level monster. These monsters can rip apart a party of characters fairly easily.

A monster of extreme threat level is a danger to even a highly experienced group of characters. These monsters should only be used at the end of a campaign or as the main enemy a group of characters face over a long series of adventures. They are not for the faint of heart!

Monsters by Threat Level

Low

- Brownie
- Dryad
- Giant Bat
- Giant Rat
- Goblin
- Kobold
- Leprechaun
- Pixie
- Skeleton
- Will-o'-the-wisp
- Zombie

Normal

- Bandit
- Bear

- Beastman
- Boar
- Carnivorous Plant
- Caveman
- Centaur
- Crocodile
- Doppelganger
- Dwarf
- Eagle
- Elf
- Gargoyle
- Ghoul
- Giant Centipede
- Giant Wolf
- Gnome
- Gorilla
- Hobgoblin
- Horse
- Merman
- Minotaur
- Nymph
- Ogre
- Orc
- Panther
- Pegasus
- Satyr
- Slaver
- Soldier
- Tiger
- Warhound
- Werewolf
- Wolf

HIGH
- Banshee
- Basilisk
- Black Knight
- Cockatrice
- Cyclops
- Dragonman
- Giant Eagle
- Giant Scorpion
- Giant Snake
- Giant Spider
- Golem
- Gorgon
- Harpy
- Hell Hound
- Hippogriff

- Lion
- Rakshasa
- Sea Serpent
- Troll
- Unicorn
- Wraith
- Yeti

Very High
- Assassin
- Catoblepas
- Chimera
- Elemental
- Genie
- Giant
- Griffon
- Hydra
- Lich
- Mammoth
- Manticore
- Phoenix
- Sphinx
- Vampire
- Wyvern

Extreme
- Angel
- Demon
- Dragon
- Kraken
- Titan
- Treeman

Terrain Types

The second list separates the different monsters into their typical native climates. Again this is helpful in picking the right monsters for the right adventure location. You wouldn't want the characters to run into bear in the middle of the desert, for instance!

A monster within the any climate list can be found anywhere. Feel free to add these monsters to your adventure no matter the setting.

Desert

Deserts are typically areas of sandy plains or dunes, but can also include rocky wastes. Basically, anywhere that is hot during the day and receives very little rainfall.

Dungeon

Dungeons include any underground area, whether they are natural caves or man-made. Many adventures take place in the numerous dungeon complexes found throughout the world.

Forest

A forest is anywhere with lots of trees in a temperate climate.

Jungle

A jungle, on the other hand, is anywhere with lots of trees in a tropical climate. Jungles are usually moist and humid and are host to a variety of dangerous creatures.

Mountains

Mountains include not only great, snow-capped peaks but also smaller mountains and foothills. Note that some mountainous areas may also be forested, and so a mixture of the two climates could apply.

Ocean

The ocean is obvious. The creatures listed here will not be encountered anywhere other than in the ocean.

Plains

An area referred to as plains is usually a large, open area of flat land or low, rolling hills. It is usually devoid of vegetation except for grass and scrub, though farmlands are also common.

Swamps

Swamps are any areas of soft, wet ground, such as bogs, marshes and fens.

Tundra

Tundra is large areas of plains covered in ice, normally only found in the polar regions of the world. Though uninhabited for the most part, some creatures thrive there.

Urban

An urban climate refers to towns and cities mostly, though also castles, villages and other settlements.

Finally, a creature listed as having a wilderness climate can be found anywhere except for dungeons, ocean and urban climates.

Monsters by Climate

Any
- Angel
- Assassin
- Bandit
- Banshee
- Black Knight
- Cyclops
- Demon
- Doppelganger
- Lightning Dragon
- Dwarf
- Elemental
- Genie
- Golem
- Horse
- Lich
- Rakshasa
- Skeleton
- Slaver
- Soldier
- Sphinx
- Vampire
- Warhound
- Wraith
- Zombie

Desert
- Giant Scorpion
- Manticore

Dungeons
- Dark Dragon
- Giant Bat
- Giant Centipede
- Giant Rat
- Giant Spider
- Goblin
- Gorgon
- Hell Hound
- Hobgoblin
- Kobold
- Minotaur
- Orc

Forest
- Bear
- Boar
- Brownie
- Carnivorous Plant
- Centaur

- Chimera
- Cockatrice
- Forest Dragon
- Dryad
- Elf
- Gargoyle
- Giant Centipede
- Giant Spider
- Giant Wolf
- Gnome
- Leprechaun
- Ogre
- Orc
- Pixie
- Satyr
- Treeman
- Unicorn
- Werewolf
- Wolf

Jungle
- Carnivorous Plant
- Forest Dragon
- Gorilla
- Manticore
- Panther
- Tiger

Mountains
- Bear
- Chimera
- Fire Dragon
- Eagle
- Gargoyle
- Giant
- Giant Eagle
- Giant Wolf
- Griffon
- Ogre
- Orc
- Pegasus
- Phoenix
- Titan
- Wolf
- Wyvern
- Yeti

Ocean
- Kraken
- Leviathan
- Merman

- Sea Serpent

Plains
- Centaur
- Lion
- Pegasus

Swamps
- Catoblepas
- Crocodile
- Hydra
- Troll
- Will-o'-the-Wisp

Tundra
- Ice Dragon
- Mammoth
- Yeti

Urban
- Ghoul
- Giant Centipede
- Giant Rat
- Werewolf

Wilderness
- Basilisk
- Beastman
- Caveman
- Dragonman
- Giant Snake
- Harpy
- Hippogriff
- Kobold

Appendix II

Treasure Generator

This final section of the Bestiary allows you to generate treasure for slain monsters. Although there is a treasure generator in the QUERP Rulebook, the Bestiary uses a different method.

As you will have seen every monster has an entry for treasure in its description. These entries – none, sparse, common, rich, wealthy, lair 1, 2 or 3 – have spate methods for generating the treasure found. Consult the following lists to find out what treasure, if any, the monster carries.

Note: Within the entries you will see things such as '1 in 6 chance' or '3 in 6 chance'. What this means is that you should roll a dice to see whether or not the monster has treasure of that type. You need to roll equal to or less than the first number listed for the monster to have treasure of that type.

None

- This monster does not possess any treasure.

Sparse

- 1-6 copper coins (1 dice)
- Basic weapons, tatty armour and mundane items such as small wooden objects, rat skulls, etc.

Common

- 1-6 silver coins (1 dice)
- 2-12 copper coins (2 dice)
- 1 in 6 chance of having 1-6 gold coins (1 dice)
- General weapons and armour

Rich

- 1-6 gold coins (1 dice)
- 3-18 silver coins (3 dice)
- 5-30 copper coins (5 dice)
- 3 in 6 chance of 1 gem
- 1 in 6 chance of 1 magic item

Wealthy

- 3-18 gold coins (3 dice)
- 5-30 silver coins (5 dice)
- 10-60 copper coins (10 dice)
- 1 gem, plus 3 in 6 chance of 1-6 other gems
- 3 in 6 chance of 1 magic item

Lair 1

- 30-180 gold coins (3 dice x 10)
- 100-600 silver coins (1 dice x 100)
- 1000-6000 copper coins (1 dice x 1000)
- 1-6 gems (1 dice)
- 1 magic item, plus 1 in 6 chance of another magic item

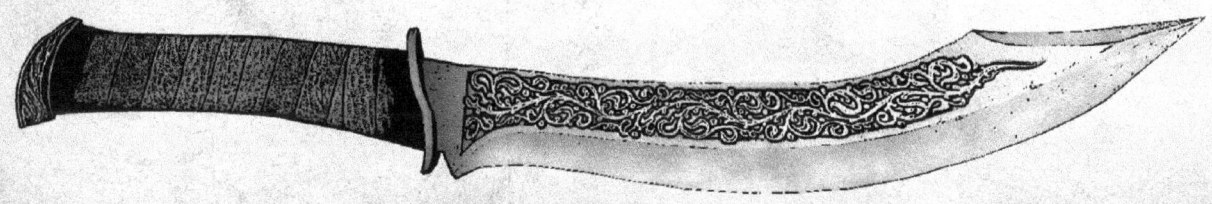

Lair 2

- 100-600 gold coins (1 dice x 100)
- 500-3000 silver coins (5 dice x 100)
- 2000-12000 copper coins (2 dice x 1000)
- 2-12 gems (2 dice)
- 1-3 magic items (1 dice divided by 2)

Lair 3

- 200-1200 gold coins (2 dice x 100)
- 1000-6000 silver coins (1 dice x 1000)
- 10000-60000 copper coins (1 dice x 10000)
- 3-18 gems (3 dice)
- 1-6 magic items (1 dice)

If the treasure indicates a magic item has been found, roll 2 dice and consult the following table to find out what kind of magic item it is, then roll on the appropriate table in the QUERP Rulebook.

2. Miscellaneous
3. Wand
4. Weapon
5. Armour
6. Potion
7. Scroll
8. Potion
9. Armour
10. Weapon
11. Wand
12. Miscellaneous

Milton Keynes UK
Ingram Content Group UK Ltd.
UKHW030850180424
441286UK00003B/27